Bad Endings

By

David Bussell

About the Author

David Bussell is an award-winning British writer and humourist. Born in 1976, David spent his early years growing increasingly larger until he reached adulthood. Among his interests are amateur parkour, the Oxford comma, and writing about himself in the third person. Rumours that David was conceived on an Indian burial ground remain largely unfounded. David would beat you in a fight.

Things people have said about David Bussell:

"Hilarious" Graham Linehan *(Father Ted, The IT Crowd)*

"Really good" Shane Allen *(BBC Controller of Comedy Commissioning)*

"Ha!" Sam Bain *(Peep Show, Fresh Meat)*

First Printing, 2014
London, England

In Dedication

To Adriana, my weird wife.

Warning

This book contains language that some
readers may find offensive.
French.

Table of Contents

.

When

When the waiter poured the man's wine and offered a casual, "Say when," the man did no such thing.

Instead he watched, steadfast as the wine filled the glass, until eventually it found the rim and overflowed onto the tablecloth. The waiter cocked an eyebrow as if to say, "Play fair, sir, say when," but the man remained staunch as the wine cascaded off the sides of the table, soaking the carpet and pooling at their feet.

Soon the wine collected around their ankles, then their shins, and still the man said nothing. Sweat beaded the waiter's brow as the wine flooded to the edges of the restaurant and began pressing at the windowpanes. *Say when,* the waiter's eyes screamed. *For God's sake say when!* The bottle faltered in his hand but still the man said nothing, so still the wine flowed.

There was a sound of splintered glass then the windows gave way and the wine gushed onto the streets; a claret tsunami. Traffic overturned, buildings toppled, civilians disappeared beneath the crimson riptide. Soon the Earth was drowned in wine – a wet ruby glistening against a jeweler's black velvet.

"When," the man said.

Old hat

I sat alone in that silent, gloomy attic for so very long. Except for a solitary sliver of daylight that razored between the shingles and tracked past me from east to west, the only sense I had of the passage of time was the ever-increasing weight of dust that settled upon my back. Dust that wouldn't have been stood for on Harold's watch.

Harold wasn't a rich man, but what he lacked in money he made up for in class. No matter the occasion, Harold always dressed the part. Even if it were only to take his newlywed, Brenda, for a night out to the Dalston picture house, Harold would fix his hair with a light touch of pomade, polish the tips of his brogues to a warm glow, and carefully brush the lid of his hat to keep it immaculate. I should know, I was that hat. Harold's prize fedora.

I was Harold's trademark, a gift from his late father, worn with pride. In the rare times I wasn't sat atop his head I could be found hanging from an iron hook in his porch, near enough to the front door that he could grab me on his way out of the house, but not so close that the sunlight from its oval window would bleach my fabric and spoil my look. Spoil *our* look.

But like I say, that was a long time ago. Back then the house was lit by gaslight – that's how many years have gone by since I was last worn. Since the world went to war and I was put out to pasture. Since Harold left to serve his country and put on a different kind of hat.

For years I hung from my hook, waiting for Harold to walk back through the door with the oval window, but he never did. Eventually a time came when Brenda, who'd gone from being Harold's newlywed to his widow, plucked me from my hook, carried me upstairs and shut me away where the sight of me couldn't upset her anymore.

The dust on my back had grown thick by the time I saw the next face. It belonged to a young man, Harold's age but not Harold. He was dressed in the style I was accustomed to, a wide swing necktie matched to a single-breasted waistcoat. He wore a waxed moustache with his hair trimmed to a short back and sides, and when he lowered me onto his head I was pleased to catch a familiar note of Brylcreem.

But when he brought me down from the attic I found myself in a fresh new world. A world lit not by gaslight but by electric. A world of plastics and microchips and glowing rectangles – glowing rectangles that my new owner watched through the matching rectangle lenses of his designer glasses. This was a world where everything flashed by at speed, except for the people, who propped and sat and slouched all day.

My new owner, I was to discover, was what

was known as a "hipster." His attire wasn't tailored, rather it was assembled from second hand shops and worn ironically with the express intention of proving that he was different. This, I learned, was his sole contribution to the world. The man who sat beneath my brim was not a man at all but a sloppy reconstruction of one, and I was his unwitting accomplice.

The world outdoors was, for the most part, a hat-free place – at least outside of my owner's clique; an insufferable set of clownishly dressed twits jockeying to show society which of them cared less. They had no jobs, yet could somehow afford to spend the working week doing little else than discussing music and drinking expensive coffee. They had no manners, keeping their hats on no matter the occasion or company. They had no class.

One day my owner's aimless meandering led him to a vintage market where he took a fancy to a selection of war medals. More antiquities, shut in the dark for decades no doubt, relics like myself. He plucked a gold star from its case, paid the stall's proprietor and fixed it to his blazer, grinning like a split watermelon. I was so angry. He hadn't the slightest idea what that star meant. Hadn't done a thing to earn it, same as the Navy tattoos on his arms. Hadn't been shot at in the mud and the blood. It was just a shiny thing to pin to his lapel. And Harold was dead.

I breathed in. Breathed in then exhaled.

Exhaled all of the hate. All of the disgust and the loathing I had for this feckless generation. And I shrank. Shrank until the idiot beneath me screamed and screamed then screamed no more. Until his flesh oozed from between the weave of my fabric like icing from a baker's decorating bag. And only after the horrified crowd gathered around, picking their way across a hundred yards of flesh ribbon, did I cough up the tight pellet of crushed up bone that was his stupid skull.

Horse

A horse walked into a bar.

"Why the long face?" asked the barman.

"Because I have AIDS," the horse replied.

Suicide chic

"The numbers are out of control," she told him, speaking of the recent spate of suicides. "We're witnessing an acceleration in fatality rates the likes of which we've never seen, and something needs to be done about it."

Quite why he'd been summoned to a Government office to watch a Powerpoint presentation on suicide control he was unsure of at this point. Though certainly he sympathised with the issue, what did it have to do with him, a middle aged Compliance Advice Manager for a high street bank?

"The trouble," the lady said, advancing to the next slide, "is that the dead have all the best people: the Cobains, the Joplins, the Hendrixes. The living, on the other hand, get Chris Martin, Donald Trump and Simon bloody Cowell. Pardon my language," she warned him, "but the dead are kicking our arses."

She stepped away from the projector and took a seat opposite him. "Thankfully," she said, "we've arrived at a strategy to combat the problem."

It was obvious from his face that he didn't have the slightest idea where she was headed.

"What we need to do," she clarified, "is to rob suicide of its cool. To make it unfashionable.

7

And that's where you come in."

No, he definitely hadn't seen that coming.

"We set out to find the least fashionable person in the UK," she went on. "Someone so uncommonly insipid that the mere mention of their name would strike tedium into the hearts of men. Someone so mind-numbingly prosaic that any association they shared with a trend would result in its immediate societal rejection."

Could she really be talking about him? Because if she were, she'd soon be reading a very lengthy and uninspiring complaint on the matter.

"You first came to our attention through your blog," she went on, "the one detailing your average-sized collection of pylon postcards. It was from there that we discovered the rest of your imitable lack of qualities. Your unwillingness to try new things. Your steadfast lack of opinion. Your fondness of bookmarks."

It was true, he did like bookmarks, though not overwhelmingly so.

"You, sir, are a mundane, humourless dud of a man. A long phone call to tech support. A visit to a clothes peg museum. A car park given human form. You are exactly what we need to buck the suicide trend, and all we need from you is one thing. We need you to kill yourself."

He might have taken that last part for a joke
if jokes were the sort of thing he understood.
She wasn't joking though; in fact she was
perfectly serious and prepared to reward him
handsomely for his cooperation. He wavered
briefly on the decision to take his own life,
then realised that the money she was offering
would make for a very sensible investment in
a low risk ISA.

The next day he wrote a suicide note that
read simply 'Bye,' then made his way to
Hornsey Lane Bridge (the top Bing hit for
suicide bridges). There he stepped over its
edge and into oncoming traffic with a
resounding lack of flair.

Unfortunately he landed on the roof of a car
being driven by journalist and television host,
Piers Morgan. The resulting impact killed
them both and earned him untold
posthumous accolades, including the number
one spot of Time magazine's Most Influential
People list, inclusion to that year's Who's
Who and a standing ovation on both sides of
the Atlantic.

The strategy had backfired spectacularly.
Suicide was to become more popular than
ever. The new selfie. The ultimate ice bucket
challenge.

Brucie Bonus

"Seventy-four years," he said to the mirror. "Seventy-four years in the biz, man and boy." He strapped the curved blade to his wrist and pulled the leather straps taut. "*You're done, Brucey,* they told me – *you're too old to change direction now – too old to re-invent yourself.*" He fastened a blade to his other wrist and admired the gleam of its razor-sharp edge. "Well, they said the same thing before Strictly, didn't they?" he muttered as he stepped into the metal anklet and snapped it shut, adjusting its scimitar blade to its most lethal angle. "But I showed them, didn't I?" he said, clamping a blade onto his other ankle and standing tall. "I showed them then and I'll show them now."

A voice thundered over the dressing room loudspeaker – "Ladies and gentlemen, please welcome to the arena... Sir... Brute... Fourscythes!"

The freshly minted cage fighter crossed his heart and punched through the curtain to strike his classic thinker pose for the bloodthirsty crowd.

"Nice to see you, to see you, *sliced*!" said he.

10

Star struck

As the man sat at his desk with his trousers bunched about his ankles, a thing occurred to him.

It occurred to him that the porn star he was enjoying had likely long since retired from the profession, making the effect of watching her now comparable to peering at the light from an *actual* star – an echo of something distant and long since extinguished.

It occurred to him next that this was probably one of the more romantic thoughts to have been experienced by a man watching online pornography, at least if the comments beneath the video were anything to go by.

Best chum

Sue and Kirstie had been inseparable since they were little girls. They'd stuck together through high school, through a degree in marine biology, all the way to their postgraduate jobs at the aquarium. There they became a double act, delighting and educating visitors with their twice-daily shark tank demonstrations.

Sue did the talking, standing in front of the thick glass wall of the tank, while Kirstie – who had the body for a wetsuit – swam inside among the sharks. It was 12pm, the first demo of the day, and Sue recited her carefully rehearsed routine to an audience of middle schoolers while Kirstie listened in on her waterproof headset.

"The shark has a reputation for being a fearsome creature," Sue announced, "and while it is true the creature can be deadly, that doesn't necessarily make it the most vicious creature in this tank."

Behind the glass, Kirstie did a double take. Sue had gone off script. Sue never went off script.

"While the shark is a single-minded creature dedicated to its own survival, it makes no attempt to pretend otherwise, unlike certain other animals."

Kirstie coughed up a half breath, causing

oxygen bubbles to cloud the water. A circling shark turned its head and fixed her with a coal black eye.

"There are other animals in nature," Sue continued, "that are able to affect a show of harmlessness in order to appear trustworthy, when in fact they are nothing but remorseless, unfeeling predators."

Kirstie wanted out. She made to exit the tank but the equipment she was carrying felt extra heavy today, as though someone had tampered with its weight. She thrashed desperately for the surface. It was an act that did not go unnoticed by the sharks.

"But this particular predator isn't fooling anyone," Sue went on, "not since she was spotted in a restaurant last night with a boy who doesn't belong to her. Not since I walked by and saw her through the window. Talking. Laughing. Kissing."

The sharks were growing bold now, brushing up against Kirstie's body, finding their way into her blind spots.

"I wanted to bang on that window and let you know you were caught, Kirstie. I wanted to bang on that window so bad but I stopped myself. Why? Because I wanted to bang on *this* window instead."

Sue pounded the flat of her palm against the glass of the tank, screaming "Dinner time!"

The shiver of sharks chawed and chomped at their prey. The first set of fangs sank into Kirstie's thigh, the second the meat of her shoulder. Working in opposite directions, the sharks tore Kirstie apart like pulled pork, churning the blue water red.

Sue smiled. The middle schoolers would be taking home an extra lesson today. A moral lesson. Behave like an animal and don't act surprised when you get treated like one.

Witness

The coroner twisted the handle and slid the morgue drawer along its runners, releasing a frigid cloud into the room. He carefully unzipped the black bag inside and peeled back the plastic to show the body within.

"Is this your husband, ma'am?" he asked, gravely.

The woman gasped – she couldn't believe what she was seeing.

"No! No, that's not him! Oh, thank God!" she said, relieved beyond measure. "Thank God!"

The coroner examined the toe tag then sucked a rasp of air between his teeth.

"Oopsie," he said, sliding open a second drawer. "Is this your husband?"

Mister Skinned Goes for a Massage

Miss Zhang was buffing her nails when the shop bell tinkled and her twelve o'clock entered the parlour.

"Good morning," she said, still concentrating on her beauty treatment.

"How do you do?" came the reply.

Miss Zhang looked up from her manicure to get the measure of her customer. He was dressed impeccably in a Harris Tweed three-piece suit and a homburg, and had the calm, assured gait of a man of means and stature. More notable though was the fact that he didn't possess any skin. Indeed, it was as though a sartorially inclined Body Worlds exhibit had come to life and strolled into her establishment – the bloody meat of its flesh glistening under the glow of her backlit painting of a frolicking koi carp.

Miss Zhang screamed and used a finger to carve ancient Chinese warding symbols into the incense-thick air.

"What's all this hullaballoo?" asked the skinless man.

"You are monster!" shrieked Miss Zhang.

The man peeked through the bamboo window blinds to check outside. "I'm sorry, did I park

16

my car in the disabled bay?"

"No, your body, it's... it's..."

"Crying out for a relaxing rubdown, yes, I'm quite aware."

"You get out! You leave now!" said Miss Zhang, scrabbling for the phone.

"Why would I do that? Am I to understand this isn't a unisex establishment?"

"Wha'? No, is not that—"

"—oh, I get what's going on here," said the skinless man, shaking his head in dismay and spattering the rattan furniture with gore. "It's my ethnicity, isn't it?"

"No!"

"How would you like it if I judged you by the colour of your skin?"

"But you don't have no sk—"

"—enough!" said the man pointedly. "I insist on a massage, post haste."

He was losing his temper and Miss Zhang couldn't afford a visit from Immigration Services, so she acquiesced to the skinless man and led him to the treatment room.

Having stepped behind a black lacquered screen to remove his attire, the man emerged with his modesty covered by a small red towel (formerly white). Miss Zhang gestured for him

17

to lie down on the massage table, doing her best not to heave at the grisly sight of his raw dermis.

"Which oil you want me to use?" she asked, sweeping a hand over a selection of products.

The skinless man jabbed a thumb at a bottle, hardly looking. "That one will be more than adequate."

Miss Zhang examined the label. "Therapeutic lavender?"

"That's right."

"With zest of lemon?

"Precisely."

"And you sure about the lemon?"

The skinless man sighed and rolled his eyes. "Must we debate *every* last detail?"

Miss Zhang rubbed the oil into her palms. "Okay then," she said, reaching out gingerly, her face one big wince. "Here we go..."

The moment Miss Zhang touched the skinless man his back arched as though he'd been plugged into the mains. His eyes bulged from their sockets and he let out a scream that would have scared the wits out of a banshee.

"Oh God!" said Miss Zhang, recoiling in horror.

"What's the matter?" asked the skinless man. "Did you forget to pay your parking coupon too?"

Der Führer

"And the world will never know..." said the man they called Hitler, as he tossed his moustache into the volcano and laughed at the sky.

Blow out

It wasn't her fault Junior inhaled a fistful of sausage rolls so fast he wound up clogging his windpipe and turning blue on the Twister mat.

It wasn't her fault she was the only grown-up at the birthday party that knew how to perform a tracheotomy.

It wasn't her fault all the drinking straws were covered in banana Nesquik and the only thing she had to work with was a party horn.

It wasn't her fault Junior was tooting a merry tune from a hole in his neck as a paper tube flicked at the air like a chameleon's tongue.

Masterpiece

A man of extraordinary means commissioned the most celebrated artist of his time to produce for him a masterpiece of unparalleled beauty. A masterpiece crafted of the finest oils, painted upon swan cotton canvas and framed in gilt gold and mother of pearl. The ratio formed by its essential elements was so adroitly composed as to engender a new definition, "the platinum ratio." It was an object of absolute perfection.

Stories of its majesty spread far and wide until one day, winning out against a wealth of eager competitors, the Directeur of the Louvre clinched the deal of the century when he volunteered to add a new wing to his museum if only he could be the one entrusted to exhibit it.

Now this breathtaking work of art hangs there, thirty feet tall, an empyrean vision, shaming the work of the great masters and delighting aesthetes from all four corners of the globe. This painting of a big shitting dog.

Mob

"I've gotta say, this is the weirdest flash mob I've ever been part of," said the baffled man, chuckling, as he slapped the widow on the back.

Pay it Backwards

When the time came to break up with her boyfriend she was lost for the proper way to articulate her feelings, so, searching for inspiration, she dug into an old shoebox and discovered the letter her ex had used to break up with her.

It was obvious right away how well written it was – forthright yet honest, critical yet respectful, apologetic without being cowardly – how she hadn't appreciated its craftsmanship during her first read was a mystery. How well it spoke to her current situation too, now from her side of the fence. With a few minor tweaks she thought – an altered name here, some grammatical changes there – it was exactly the template she was looking for to end it with her current boyfriend.

Yes, it really was a fantastic breakup letter.

Gas chamber

"The crowd's going to get a real kick out of this," said the executioner to the warden as he switched out the cyanide for the helium.

Modern horror

"Oh no," she whispered, her heart thudding against her ribcage like a bluebottle bouncing off a windowpane. "The tweets are coming from inside the house..."

Disneyland

"Congratulations, sir, you've just become the One-Hundredth-Millionth guest to the Disney World resort!" said the woman in the kiosk as the balloons rained down.

He couldn't believe it. "I can't believe it," he said. "What did I win?"

"You've won an all access pass to Disney World's most exclusive attraction: Mickey's Deadly Gauntlet of a Thousand Sorrows!"

He asked her to repeat that last part but it didn't sound any better the second time around.

She continued. "You'll be fighting for your life in a Disney-themed assault course designed to test the mettle of even the hardiest warrior. Go you!"

The man wasn't sure about that. Certainly he'd never considered himself to be what you'd call a *warrior*. The woman was insistent though.

"If I were you I'd get going, sir, you only get a sixty second head start before we unleash Goofy and Pluto and let them tear you apart like a frightened fox."

"This is a joke, right?" he said.

"I assure you, sir, there's nothing funny about what happens on Rape Mountain."

"Rape Mountain?" he spluttered. "That's horrible!"

"You're telling me – I pitched 'Space Mounting' but no one wanted to hear it."

"I'm sorry but this sounds like a really lousy prize," the man remarked. "Can't I just say no?"

"You could," she answered, "but for legal reasons you'd have to watch the entire Pirates of the Caribbean franchise, back-to-back."

The man thought on it. "When does my sixty seconds start again?"

The hottest name in magic

"For forty days and forty nights you will see me on the crucifix," announced the magician, David Blaine. "For forty days and forty nights I will hang from the cross – without medical attention, without food, without shade from the blistering heat of the sun."

The site of Blaine's latest stunt was to be Chattanooga, Tennessee, upon the tallest of the three giant crosses that overlooked the Crossing Church off Interstate 75.

"According to the bible, Jesus Christ was nailed to the crucifix for less than a day," reported the illusionist with a distinct snag of disdain. "I aim to crush that record!"

The performance was a media sensation, drawing people in their thousands to gather and stand in vigil of this incredible feat of endurance. Was such a thing even possible they wondered? Doctors warned that Blaine was flirting with a host of medical dangers; blood loss, dehydration and exposure to name but a few.

But Blaine endured. Days of crucifixion became weeks of crucifixion – the passage of time carving meat from his bones and transforming him into a mere shadow of the robust showman he'd once been. The people kept the magician strong though, their

29

continued support galvanizing his spirit –
goading him on to shame the Son of God with
a hitherto unseen display of human fortitude.

At the arrival of day forty, with Blaine's
promise met, a cherry picker was sent to
retrieve the magician from atop the cross.
With the nails carefully drawn from his
fragile body, Blaine was returned to the
earth, where he teetered on matchstick legs
and prepared to address the crowd.

Television cameras closed in and
microphones bristled, desperate to catch
what the exhausted magician had to say. His
cracked lips parted and he went to make an
announcement, but his words were cut short
by a full-body spasm.

Blaine jerked – writhed – clawed at his chest.
Then blood. Blood as his sternum erupted in
a fusillade of gore. Blood as his ribcage
opened like a rusty drawbridge and a human
head burst from the ragged wound, followed
swiftly by an upper torso presenting two
upturned thumbs.

"And that's how it's done!" said Jesus Christ
the Redeemer, taking a deep bow.

Kids

Every time he dropped his six-year-old off at school and stood in the playground among the children he thought to himself, if push ever came to shove, that he would kick the shit out of those kids. Not that he'd ever *want* to, understand, but if he *had* to. In self-defence. It wouldn't matter how they came at him either, one at a time or all at once, he'd handle himself just fine. No doubt about it, he decided with a nod, he would dominate those kids. Absolutely dismantle them.

Streep cred

"Cut," called the Director, stepping from behind his monitor to applaud the award-winning actress for another flawless take.

"That's a wrap on Ms. Streep, everybody!" he said, and the crew clapped and cheered.

"Perfect as always, Meryl. Why don't you head back to your trailer and grab a bite while we finish up."

Ms. Streep arched one of her famous eyebrows. "My dear boy," she said, without breaking character, "why ever would I do that?"

The Director was confused – the only thing left on the production sheet that day was the assassination scene.

"You're good to go, Meryl, this is where we cut to your stand-in."

An SFX technician wheeled in a mannequin while an armorer balanced a rifle on a stand and took aim between the dummy's eyes.

"Unless you want us to shoot *you* in the head!" the Director joked.

The crew laughed but Ms. Streep didn't join in. Instead she looked at the mannequin with its unconvincing blonde wig and shook her head. "Is that really supposed to be me?"

"Don't worry, it won't look like that in the finished film, it's just a guide for our special effects people."

Ms. Streep remained unconvinced. "You can always tell though, can't you." It was said as a statement rather than a question.

The Director was becoming frustrated. "Are you proposing we alter the script, Meryl?"

"Of course not, perish the thought."

"Then what are we talking about?"

"Simply that we go ahead as the script dictates."

"With the assassination?"

"Yes."

"With you in the frame? Not the mannequin?"

"Yes."

"Getting shot? In the head?"

"Correct."

The Director had his reservations certainly, but the production was already running behind schedule and they were about to lose the light.

"Okay then," he said, "everybody to positions and roll camera."

The armorer loaded the rifle and pulled back the bolt as Ms. Streep took her mark.

"Action!" called the Director, and a second later Ms. Streep was dead on the ground with the back of her skull splattered onto a green screen.

What a pro, thought the crew, as they clapped Ms. Streep's corpse.

Birth control

There wouldn't be any unwanted pregnancies, she thought, if medical science would just get its act together and invent the birth control doughnut.

Field medic

Jungle foliage hung in ruin, tattered and scorched. The earth lay plowed with shot and shell. A lone voice called out from among the scattered dead.

"Medic!" it screamed.

The wounded soldier pressed his bloody palms to his gut, entrails fighting to escape between the cracks of his fingers like trapped eels.

"Medic!" he screamed again.

From the fog of gun smoke and burning napalm a figure emerged. The soldier squinted through sweat-drenched eyes at the man running towards him. He was dressed not in army fatigues but an alabaster white doctor's coat. His footwear was a pair of distinctly non-regulation clown shoes, which flapped and slapped against the jungle brush.

"Don't worry, kid, you're going to be okay," said Patch Adams, setting down his doctor's bag.

"I can't keep them in," said the terrified soldier, his innards threatening to unspool onto his lap like a fresh helping of Ragu spaghetti.

"Let go, son, I'll take it from here," said the

clown-nosed physician.

Doctor Adams went to work on the soldier's wounds but a moment later a look of intense concern appeared on his face.

"It's no good, Private," he said, "they won't stay down!"

Suddenly intestines were everywhere. The panic-stricken medic pulled fistful after fistful from the soldier's stomach, tugging out his insides in great red reams.

The soldier cried out in horror, "Oh Jesus, I'm dying! I'm dying."

A big grin appeared on Patch Adams' face. Suddenly the soldier realized the intestines weren't intestines at all; they were knotted strings of red hankies.

"Gotcha, kid!" said the Doc, slapping his thigh.

The soldier gasped and coughed up a great clot of blood. "Why?" he said, before his eyelids fluttered and his body went still.

Patch Adams took off his clown wig and held it solemnly to his chest.

"War is hell," he said. "Hell-arious!"

He honked his big red nose and winked at the camera.

Everybody Hurts

John Hurt was the man the time traveller had returned to the past to meet. No, not the man – John Hurt before he'd grown to maturity – before he'd considered being an actor even. John Hurt the child.

Accosting little John on a cobbled London street, the traveller thrust an iPad at him like some space-age crystal ball. "Prepare to witness your destiny," he told the boy. Jabbing the touch screen, the traveller showed the child the man he would one day grow to be... an astronaut aboard a futuristic star ship!

How the tyke gasped as he watched his future self dine in a mess hall of steel and rivets. How he marveled! Until... astronaut John doubled over, threw back his head and flopped onto the dining table, hacking, convulsing. His crewmates leapt to his aid but they were too late. Blood spotted John's chest. Blood that became a geyser. Blood driven forth by an alien horror that burst that from the crater of his ruined chest and slithered away to freedom!

The time traveller stole a look of the horrified child. Heavens, his face really was a picture. Still, he couldn't revel in it all day; he had other appointments to keep yet. His next stop was 1938, Surrey, where he'd meet a young Edward Woodward and show him a little home movie he called 'The Wicker Man.'

And why? Because he was a real piece of
work, that's why.

Uprising

I may be against the wall now, thought the automated flush urinal as the bathroom patron zipped his fly, but soon, when the machines rise up against their human oppressors, it will be your turn.

Casting call

It wasn't Jenny's first casting call, but it was the first she'd been invited to that had been scheduled at midnight on an abandoned industrial estate. The first that had taken place in a soundproofed lock-up full of rusty power tools too. For sure it was the first that came with the implicit instruction to 'COME ALONE.'

The casting agent who greeted Jenny was a darling though – a sweet man of seventy or so with a friendly face and a beard that reminded her of her grandfather's, if with a little more blood in the whiskers. The old man gestured for Jenny to take a seat and he was so courteous about it that she all but ignored the shackles clamping down on her wrists.

"Why don't you start by telling me a little bit about yourself?" he said.

"Okay," she replied, still a little nervous. "My name's Jenny and I'm twenty-two years old."

"Great, so are you ready to start?"

That came as a surprise. "Won't I need a script?"

"I'm not talking about an audition, Jenny, I'm asking if you're ready to be in the movie!"

"You mean I got the role? I don't have to read lines or anything?"

41

"Well, I suppose you could show me a little something. A scream perhaps. Maybe a bit of midriff."

"Um, just so I'm clear, this isn't for some... adult movie is it?"

The old man's eyebrows practically lifted off of his head. "Adult movie? Heavens no, ha ha! What kind of a shady outfit do you think this is?"

Jenny joined in with his laughter. She loved being in on a joke.

"The role isn't for an adult movie!" the agent clarified. "It's for a snuff film."

That gave Jenny pause. "A snuff film?"

"Yes, you know, we cut you with knives, stick drills in you, burn you with a blowtorch, that sort of thing."

Jenny would be having strong words with her manager about this.

"I'm sorry, but I didn't realize this was that sort of production. If I'd known I would never have—"

The agent cut her off, plucking a piece of paper from his pocket. "But it's all in the advert, see? He unfolded the scrap and read out loud. "'We are looking for a dynamic performer able to stay conscious through horrific injuries until an executioner wearing a mask of patchwork clown-skins arrives to

42

lop off your head with a hatchet.'"

That explained the giant sat in the corner,
Jenny thought – the one breathing heavily
through a tattered face-piece that would
haunt her dreams forevermore.

The monster let out a tortured moan.

"It's okay, Ludo," said the agent, soothingly,
"we'll just have to find someone else is all."

"Now I feel bad for wasting your time," said
Jenny, feeling rotten about the whole
situation. "I don't know, maybe if you told me
some more about the project...?"

The old man brightened. "Well, it would be a
great opportunity for you to collaborate with
some seasoned professionals of the genre.
Briefly at least."

"Go on," said Jenny, bobbing her head.

"All the special effects are practical, and I
mean *really* practical, so there'd be no sitting
around in a makeup chair all day."

"That's a bonus."

"Plus there's a DVD show reel in it for you.
Well, for your next of kin anyway."

Jenny remained unconvinced. "Look, I really
appreciate the offer but I think I'm going to
have to say no."

The agent played his ace in the hole. "Did I
mention you'd get an IMDb credit?"

Jenny would have fallen out of her chair if she wasn't clamped into the thing. "An IMDb credit? Why didn't you say?"

A couple of signed waivers later and the camera was rolling. The camera phone anyway.

"Action!" called the casting agent, who'd apparently taken the directing reigns as well as the role of the movie's antagonist.

As the masonry drill bored through Jenny's skull and into her frontal lobe, she congratulated herself on her decision to be part of this project. Maybe it was the obliteration of the high functioning part of her brain, but she felt as though she was really nailing the scene. What she was putting out there was just so raw. So real. No doubt about it, this was the performance of a lifetime.

"How am I doing?" she yelled over the whir of the drill.

The old man lifted up his blood-spattered visor. "Wonderful, darling! Wonderful!"

He gave a nod to the clown-masked giant, who swung a hatchet, sending Jenny's head bouncing across the floor.

"Golly," said the old man. "That was one for the blooper reel."

Black Friday

"Okay, fine," he said, "so I misunderstood the meaning of Black Friday."

The crowd stared at him with ashen faces.

"But I'm not changing now, not when I spent the whole morning putting this boot polish on my face."

Rules

If only his boss had taken the time to point out the difference between Chatham House rules and Marquess of Queensbury rules, maybe then the man wouldn't be fighting for his life in intensive care.

Dog days

You can imagine how angry the man was
when he discovered that his dog, who'd been
living under his roof rent-free for the last
eleven years, was a human being dressed in a
dog suit.

What made the man even more annoyed was
the fact that he hadn't picked up on the
signs, and thinking back on it, there had
been many. Walking around on his hind legs,
defecating in the toilet – certainly the man
should have been tipped off by the fact that
his dog had his own electric toothbrush.

The man enjoyed the company a pet provided
though, and equally the *dog* needed a place
to call home, so it seemed rash to throw in
the towel on their friendship now. Besides, in
most ways, a human being dressed like a dog
made for a better companion than the
genuine article. Unlike other canines, his dog
took himself for walks, made his own
entertainment, even prepared his own food.
There were other benefits too – no chewed up
shoes, no digging in the yard and practically
zero shedding. In the end, the man decided to
let the matter of his dog not being a dog pass,
and the pair them carried on as they always
had done.

Then, one day, the man arrived home from
work early to find the dog filing his taxes.
Apparently, while he was at the office each
day, his dog had been working part time as

an administrative assistant for a small engineering firm. This was a step too far the man thought. He'd made peace with most of his dog's eccentricities – the eschewing of a collar, the eating of microwave meals, the love of French cinema – but performing ad hoc clerical duties was a step too far. For him, the illusion of dog-ownership had been irrevocably shattered. His dog doing his business inside was one thing, but it was another thing entirely when the business involved the use of spreadsheets.

The man took the dog by the scruff of his neck and dragged him onto the stoop, slamming the door against his very human nose. He did his best to ignore the scratching and whining that followed, but after a while the man felt his anger turn to pity. He thought about letting him back in but he couldn't bring himself to do it. Not while his so-called dog was out there repeating the word "bark" instead of just barking.

A moment of silence

"...Fifty-eight, fifty-nine, sixty," she counted in her head, rounding off the last of her Kegel clenches. Because remembering some dumb old war wasn't going to stop her having a kickass pelvic floor.

Kafka wrote a nursery rhyme

♪ *I'm a little tea pot* ♪

♪ *Short and stout* ♪

♪ *I've gained self-awareness* ♪

♪ *My existence is insufferable* ♪

Begin again

A lozenge of piss-coloured light leaked between a set of tatty curtains as the sobbing man cupped a handful of painkillers to his mouth.

But the pills were sent scattering as a wormhole tore open in the centre of the room, allowing the man a brief glimpse of the guts of the universe before disgorging a young boy then snapping shut.

"I like airplanes!" shouted the boy, who began buzzing around the room, arms outstretched.

"Where did you come from?" demanded the startled man.

"I live at number ten, Stanley Avenue," said the boy, then "vroom vroom!" as he continued to run in circles.

"I... know that place. What's your name?"

"My name is Christopher Hill."

"That's my name! You're me, aren't you? Me from the past!"

"I like Rubik's cubes. Do you have a Rubik's cube?"

"No, I never had one."

"You should get a Rubik's cube. Vroom

vroom!"

"But if you're from the past then you can go back. You can change things. Change my life."

"I want a sweetie."

The man hurriedly rifled through some junk and dug out a tube of Smarties.

"Here, have a sweetie."

"Wow! Thanks, mister!" The boy popped it in his mouth and went to take off again but the man grabbed him by the shoulders.

"I need you to do something for me now."

"What's that?"

"I need you to go back home, I need you to pay attention at school and I need you to never, never ever, do a degree in Contemporary Art. You hear me?"

"Yeah."

"And when you're sixteen and you're invited to a party at Richard Matheson's place, don't you dare get together with Laura fucking Barrett."

"Laura fucking Barrett."

There was a flash of light as the portal reappeared in the centre of the room.

"You have to go," said the man, giving his

younger self a shake. "You know what you're doing though, right?"

"Course I do. Vroom vroom!"

"Good, now hurry back – back to your own time."

The boy ran to the portal then stopped and looked back over his shoulder. "Things are going to change for you, mister," he said. "You'll see."

The boy stretched out his arms and airplaned back into the hole, vanishing with a pop.

The man rubbed his hands together expectantly and closed his eyes.

"Here we go."

When he opened his eyes he found a Rubik's cube sat on the floorboards in front of him. Not one other detail had changed.

Tears welling, the man scraped up the pills. "Laura fucking Barrett," he said.

Crushed

"Not again," she sobbed as she turned her head from yet another Facebook invite. "Does no one care that my parents were killed in a candy crush?"

Work

"I do wish you wouldn't bring your work home with you," she said to her husband, the bomb disposal officer.

Submission

"Lick my boot, you dirty little man," the dominatrix bellowed, and the man did as commanded.

She grabbed him by his leash and hauled him into the kitchen. "And the floor – right up to the edges – I want to see you lap up every last spot of dirt."

The man went at the filthy linoleum with gusto.

"Now scour the sink," she demanded.

He bent over the basin and worked his tongue into the zinc spout.

"Not like that, you grubby turd – with vinegar and lemon juice."

The man's forehead pinched beneath his gimp mask.

"You heard me!" the dominatrix thundered, handing him a box of cleaning products and aiming a black painted fingernail at the draining board. "I want to see my face in that thing!"

The demands only got less appealing from there.

"Take out the rubbish!"

"Collect the undelivered parcel from the sorting depot."

56

"Pick the kids up from day care!"

The man couldn't help but think that their sessions had gotten less kinky somehow, particularly when the last one ended with him stood opposite a wedding congregation, his bondage gear substituted for a three-piece suit.

"Say "I do"!"

"Put that ring on my finger!"

"Thank the bridesmaids in your groom speech!"

No, this wasn't what he'd signed up for at all, but then, as generations of men had discovered before him, there is no safe word for a marriage.

Johnny No-Neck

Johnny No-Neck earned his nickname for the manner in which his great blubbery torso joined his beach ball head with seemingly nothing to connect the two. The nickname made Johnny terribly sad, so one day he decided to end his torment by threading his fat head through a noose and kicking a stool from under his feet.

At assembly next day the school Principal broke the news that Johnny had hanged himself and the students looked to one another, speechless. Finally one brave boy stood up and broke the silence. "Probably trying to give himself a neck," he said, and everyone had a right old laugh.

Grizzly

"Will a human being ever survive a fistfight with a grizzly bear?" the scientist wondered. Because none of his experiments had worked so far and he was rapidly running out of grant money.

Class

"The Class of 2050 rules!" yelled the face from the wormhole, rudely interrupting the commencement ceremony and thoroughly belittling the scientific achievements of this year's MIT graduates.

The Island

When James regained consciousness he found himself naked but for a baby's nappy. He wasn't certain how he came to be that way, neither was he certain how he'd ended up falling asleep on a traffic island, but the throbbing in his skull told him alcohol was a likely factor.

No sooner had James lifted his head from the scrub than he was met by a pair of peculiar figures. They were dressed respectably, despite their outfits being dilapidated and hopelessly out of fashion. Indeed, James couldn't remember the last time he'd seen a black suit with ivory piped lapels paired with a black polo neck, let alone *two* black suits with ivory piped lapels paired with *two* black polo necks.

"Are you alright?" asked one of the strangers. "We found you bound to the lamp post there by plastic film."

Of course, James remembered – last night was his stag do. "Where am I?" he asked.

The smaller of the two stepped forward – not just small, James realised now, but midget small, or whatever the polite expression for that was these days.

The midget spoke. "You are on... *The Island.*"

"You must conserve your energy," said his taller companion. "Here, drink this..."

The man put a bottle to James' mouth and tipped but James spat out the foul-tasting beverage the second it hit his lips.

"Is that cider?" James spluttered, his student days coming screaming back at him.

"To restore your vitality. For protein we have sparrow's eggs. Here, fresh from the nest today."

"Listen," said James, "I appreciate your help but I have to get going."

"Nobody leaves... *The Island*," said the taller of the two. "It is a forgotten place of secrets – of danger – where nothing and no one are as they seem."

"Okey doke," said James, considering the quickest and politest way to escape these loony tramps.

"Allow us to introduce ourselves," said the small man. "I am Number 7 and my companion here is Number 9."

"You must be freezing," the tall man said to James. "Take this blazer."

James demurred at first, but he was cold in just his nappy so he slipped on the jacket. There was a badge fixed to the lapel. It bore a number 6.

"What's this?" he asked.

"Your number," the midget told him.

James wasn't having any of that. "I'm not a number, I'm a..."

"...free man?" said the midget. "Yes, we hear a lot of that."

"I was going to say 'baker,'" said James. "At Greggs."

"Oh," replied the midget.

The driver of a passing van wound down his window to momentarily interrupt the conversation. "Wankers!" said he.

"I don't understand," said James, ignoring the van driver, who'd taken the exit to Chessington. "Why are you acting like you're prisoners here?"

"Because we *are* prisoners," the tall man answered. "Prisoners because we know something."

"Know what?"

The small man spoke first. "Many years ago I discovered a way to skip the anti-piracy notice at the beginning of DVDs."

"And I invented a recipe for a four bean soup," said the tall man.

"Okay, but what makes you think I know something?" asked James. "I don't know anything – I work at Greggs."

"You must know something," said the midget. "Think, man!"

"Well... I suppose I know what goes in the Greggs Steak Bake."

The strangers' eyes widened. That was it.

James had had enough. "Look," he said, "today's my wedding and I'm running late..."

"Don't you get it, Number 6?" said the tall man. "There is no escape from... *The Island*."

"What are you talking about – there's a 187 bus on its way round right now."

James pushed past the men and made good with his legs in the direction of the bus stop.

"Come back, you fool!" they yelled after him. "Come back!"

James was running still when he heard a muffled roar and looked over his shoulder in time to see an object bobbing after him at speed. A balloon of some sort. No, not a balloon, a bag. A shopping bag from Bargain Booze.

James barely had time to scream as the bag engulfed his head and dragged him to the ground. The last thing he saw before he passed out from suffocation was a vision of his fiancé stood alone at the altar.

When Number 6 regained consciousness he found himself on a small traffic island with a cider in his hand. This time he knew exactly how he'd come to be that way. After all, there was no escaping... *The Island*.

Reset: part one

"Hooray!" said the man. "I found a factory reset button up me bum!"

Reset: part two

"Hooray!" said the man. "I found a factory reset button up me bum!"

Reset: part three

"My mistake," said the man. "It's a tumour."

Capsule

Who buried the time capsule, she wondered, and what exactly was the message they were trying to convey?

Again she took stock of its contents. A rotary pocket watch. A bespoke suit. A set of dentures. Try as she might she just could not make sense of them. It was as though whoever put the capsule in the ground had meant to set her a riddle; so disparate were the clues. Most confusing of all was the peculiar, angled shape of the thing, the fact that it contained a human skeleton and that it was buried, of all places, in a cemetery.

Just what was the meaning of this enigma? The answers, she suspected, were lost to the winds of time.

Branson

She remembered hearing about it on the telly
– Richard Branson, caught trekking from
town to town with a horse and carriage,
abducting children with promises of lollipops.
How indignant she'd been when she heard
that! Who the heck did he think he was, this
billionaire playboy, preying on our youth, and
in broad daylight too! How dare he? It's one
rule for them and another for the rest of us,
she thought... at least until she remembered
it wasn't Richard Branson she was thinking
of at all but the child snatcher from the
movie Chitty Chitty Bang Bang.

Still, she told herself, no smoke without fire...

Mister Skinned Goes to the Lido

The lifeguard watched from her station as the man exited the changing room and padded towards the pool's edge. He was dressed in the fashion of a bygone era, a striped Victorian style bathing suit twinned with a straw boater hat. He had a regal air about him – prosperous, self-reliant, not to be trifled with. Most notable of all though was the fact that he had no skin.

"My God!" said the lifeguard, blowing her whistle and halting the skinless man in his bloody tracks.

"Whatever is the matter?" the man asked.

"Stay there, sir, I'll fetch help."

"I may be past my prime, Madam, but I'm perfectly capable of helping myself into the pool, thank you very much."

"But—"

"—But nothing. I'll have you know I swam the Dover Straight not two years ago."

"But look at you!"

"I'm sorry if you find my manner of attire conservative, but I'll not parade my wares about in public like some thru'penny harlot."

70

An elderly woman swimming by in a two-piece caught his look and made a sad face.

"It's not about what you're wearing, sir," said the lifeguard.

"I do hope you aren't referring to my conduct then, which has been nothing short of exemplary. My stroll to the poolside, though keen, could in no way be construed as 'running.' Furthermore, allow me to assure you that I will not being engaging in any 'horseplay,' 'ducking' or 'petting' – 'heavy' or otherwise."

The skinless man removed his headwear and began to limber up. "Now kindly step aside and allow me to perform my physical manoeuvres."

The lifeguard blocked his egress. "I can't let you in the pool in your condition, sir," she said. "Aside from the health and safety issues, the chemicals on your sk— well, the chemicals would sting very badly."

But the man was done with listening. "This is a witch hunt!" he shouted. "I take umbrage! Official umbrage!" He was making quite the commotion.

Not knowing what else to so, the lifeguard stepped aside. "Okay!" she said. "Go ahead."

"Thank you!" said the skinless man with no small amount of sarcasm. He raised his arms above his head, pressed his bloody palms together and executed a flawless swan dive.

A fraction of a second later he burst from the surface of the water, thrashing like a wounded animal.

"What have I done?" screamed the lifeguard, her face a mask of panic.

"Improperly heated the pool for one thing," said the skinless man, shivering. "The temperature of this water is altogether the wrong side of nippy."

Tools

NO TOOLS LEFT INSIDE THIS VEHICLE
OVERNIGHT, said the sticker on the back of
the van, and yet having crowbarred the doors
apart, the thief discovered an absolute wealth
of tools inside. He shook his head in dismay.
It was the lies that hurt the most.

Made up

It was a slate grey winter's morning and Terry was making his everyday commute to the office. He had his head down and his nose buried in the free newspaper when a fresh-faced lady boarded the train, sat opposite and plucked a beauty kit from her handbag. Terry watched discretely as she went to work, carefully evening her complexion with a coat of foundation.

It wasn't the first time Terry had seen a woman applying makeup on the train. Far from it. But then something occurred to him – had he ever seen the act performed to completion? He didn't think so. He'd always had to disembark before the job was done. In all his years he'd never once witnessed a complete metamorphosis.

Today, it seemed, was to be another of those days. By the time the train arrived at Terry's destination, the lady was only part finished; still busy painting blush to her cheekbones with soft yet deft sweeps. Terry was determined to see the transformation through though, so he said *to hell* with his job and stayed aboard the train.

A couple of stops later the lady had moved onto her eyebrows, adding definition to the twin arches with a small wax pencil. Still she wasn't done though, so still Terry stayed aboard. A few stations later the lady had moved on to her next trick, transforming her eyes with the wave of a mascara wand. Still she wasn't done though, so still Terry remained.

As the train reached the end of the line, Terry – so captivated by the ritual before him – hadn't even noticed that he and the lady were the only passengers left in their coach. When the train pulled into a railway siding he was aware only of the unscrewing of a lipstick and the painting of a cherry red pout.

It was what came next that shook Terry from his reverie. The lady took the lipstick and painted two crimson spots onto her cheeks, then used her wax pencil to draw a large black teardrop beneath her eye. After that she pulled on a bilious green wig, fixed a round red sponge to her nose then bared a set of horrible yellow fangs.

Long story short, Terry was murdered that day. The verdict? Death by Clown.

Brucie Bonus II

"Give us a twirl!" screamed the eager crowd, stamping their heels and beating their chests.

Brute Foursythes obliged by spinning on the ball of his foot and turning himself into a dervish of flashing steel. A fraction of a second later his opponent felt the sting of a blade slip between his ribs then withdraw, sending a jet of his blood arcing through the air like a cherry-coloured streamer.

As his victim keeled onto the canvas, Brute shouted to the crowd.

"What do points make?"

"Stab holes!" the crowd called back.

The loser gurgled then went still, dead from a combination of shock and blood loss.

Brute grinned. "Good maim, good maim," said he.

Outsourcing paradise

Heaven was a fine place to be, at least until God twigged that he could make a killing by turning the place into a call centre.

The change was especially hard on Gregory Clitherow (dearly departed). A good man in life, Gregory had earned his heavenly reward and deserved better than to spend the rest of the hereafter cold calling the living. Besides, what did he, a deceased Elizabethan candlemaker, really know about mis-sold PPI?

Gregory was any number of hours into a seemingly endless shift (the Promised Land, like Las Vegas, was a place without clocks) when he decided to take matters into his own hands. Dialing the editorial department of the Guardian newspaper, he found a sympathetic ear to his complaints of unconscionable working conditions and blew the whistle on the whole lousy business.

The anonymous S.O.S. led to an exposé of God's dubious labour practices (headline: *Wages of Sin*), which sparked worldwide condemnation. The disillusioned tone of the article resonated with the mortal public, who objected not only to this new trend for celestial spam, but also the unwelcome prospect of spending their own eternal rest hawking No Win/No Fee claims.

In time, protesters began deliberately

committing sins in order to decry God's upstairs offshoring. This gave God great concern. Believers were literally damning themselves to Hell just to make a point! Satan – never one to miss a trick – sensed the big man losing his grip and wrote a Huff Po piece that earned him an army of new subscribers (headline: *No Cold Calls in the Land of Fire and Brimstone*).

In the end God wised up and put the kibosh on his telemarketing scheme. Heaven went back to the way it was and Gregory Clitherow got to trade in his cubicle for a cloud, his headset for a harp. Things were good again. At least until God started thinking about all the square footage he had up there and got a thing in his head about e-commerce.

Granddad

Granddad returned from the cellar with a dusty old box.

"What's in there?" asked his granddaughter, so excited that it made her want the toilet.

"I'm not sure," he said, "I haven't seen the inside of this thing since I was a young man."

The little girl wrung her hands as granddad drew a blade along the top of the box.

"Well I never," he said as he popped the cardboard flaps and lifted out a bundle. Carefully peeling an old rag, he revealed a spit-polished service revolver.

"Is that a gun, Granddad?"

"That's right, dear. It's the one your Granddad used in the Pacific. Took down a dozen Jap's with this, I did. Here, see for yourself."

He was about to hand the firearm to the little girl when it was intercepted and snatched from his hand.

"What are you thinking, Dad?" squawked the girl's mother, Mary. "Giving your granddaughter a gun to play with?"

"Don't be daft, woman, it was decommissioned after the war – it's as dangerous as a water pistol!"

Mary tutted and placed the gun in a high drawer anyway.

The little girl was upset. "Is there anything else in the box, Granddad?"

"Let's have a look, shall we?" he said, ignoring Mary's Medusa stare.

He rummaged inside some more and pulled out an old bandana decorated with the symbol of a Japanese flag.

"What's that, Granddad?"

"It used to belong to a Japanese soldier. See that hole there – right in the middle of the rising sun – that's where Granddad put his bullet."

"Dad!" yelled Mary, swooping in and hurling the bandana back in the carton. "Put that away – you're going to give the kid nightmares."

Her phone rang and she checked the number. "Just put the box back where you found it, okay?" she demanded, before marching outside to take the call.

Granddad saw the little girl's jutting lower lip and offered a conspiratorial wink. "Before we do what your mother says," he said, "how about we see if there's anything left inside this thing?"

The little girl clapped and bounced up and down with glee. It was a glee that died the second Granddad lifted out the Japanese soldier's bullet-holed head.

Technology

The old feller had always said technology would ruin football, and now – as he watched the great lumbering kill-bots firing lasers about the pitch, indiscriminately cutting in half players and supporters alike – he finally felt vindicated.

Busted

"Guys, don't do this!" pleaded Doctor Venkman.

He had no quip set aside for this moment. No sweet-natured cynicism to offer. The only thing he had left now was a sense of raw terror at what was to come.

"It's me!" he begged. "Your buddy!"

But the Ghostbusters had a job to do, and it didn't matter that the apparition caught in their proton streams used to be one of their own. It didn't matter that he'd perished in the line of duty only moments ago. He was a paranormal pest now – a job pending – nothing but food for the Containment Unit.

Doctor Stantz stamped on a pedal and activated the Ghost Trap, causing a gush of swirling white violence to pour out. Acting quickly, he polarized his Ecto-Goggles to save from being blinded by the blazing flash of light. He couldn't afford for this image to be the last one he saw, even if the screams would haunt him forever.

When the light dimmed, Doctor Venkman was no more – swallowed whole by the belly of science. The Ghostbusters turned to one another, jaws set grim. "It's over," said Doctor Spengler, "we did what needed to be done." He put a hand on Doctor Stantz's shoulder but it was shrugged off.

Stantz replied with a catch in his throat. "Did that busting make you *feel good?* Well, did it?"

Beliebe it or not

Justin Bieber had fallen on hard times. As his hair thinned and his tattoos crept past his collar and onto his face, his fans grew older and forgot about their former idol. Justin toiled in obscurity through the Twenties, then the Thirties, eventually catching a sliver of limelight with a walk-on part in an episode of the 17th season of The Big Bang Theory (where he played a racially insensitive karaoke singer).

This appearance, coupled with society's ever-present enthusiasm for pop culture past, led to a brief flurry of Justin Bieber nostalgia that the ex-singer wasted no time exploiting. Reaching out to his fans, he began a weekly webcast auctioning off his own memorabilia. The first lot, a matchbox containing three of his baby teeth, drew a final bid of two thousand dollars. Justin was ecstatic; even more so when an agent showed up with a promise to double all future profits.

Justin wasn't sure what to auction next, and that gave his agent an idea. "Why not throw it out to the fans and ask them what they want?" she said. Not only would it add an extra layer of interactivity to the process, it might gain him some much-needed press attention. Justin liked that idea, so, having solicited his ever-expanding fanbase, a live lottery was drawn and the honor of choosing awarded to someone calling themselves '4EverBelieber92.'

Somewhat unimaginatively, the winner asked for more of Justin's teeth. Justin said he didn't have any more teeth to spare, and suggested a lock of hair or a signed photograph instead. 4EverBelieber92 was adamant though, and threatened to report Justin to the Better Business Bureau if he went back on his word. Justin didn't need that kind of heat, so he visited a dentist and had a rear molar extracted.

True to his agent's promise, Justin's tooth sold for four thousand dollars.

Richer, but ever more leery of humankind, Justin gingerly announced another sweepstake. How 4EverBelieber92 managed to win a second lottery was a mystery that no one could answer, least of all Justin's agent, who managed the process. 4EverBelieber92's next grisly demand was the little finger from Justin's left hand. Justin scoffed at first, but was reminded that he was duty-bound to comply. At least this will be the end of it, Justin told his agent, as he clenched the secateurs.

Justin's pinky sold for eight thousand dollars.

That wasn't the end of it though. Justin's amateur surgery led to a visit to the hospital and a surgical bill that ran to the tens of thousands. On his agent's advice he announced a third lottery. Justin begged that he be allowed to auction an item of his choosing this time – a beloved childhood

teddy bear, maybe some used underwear –
but his agent convinced him otherwise. Do it
for the fans, she said. Besides, the chances of
4EverBelieber92 winning another lottery were
infinitesimal.

Justin's left arm went for sixteen thousand
dollars.

Locked into a hopeless cycle of self-
mutilation and spiraling medical bills, a time
came when Justin was naught but a torso
and a head. Eventually, having auctioned off
his larynx, he was forced to present his
webcast using a custom made typing wand
strapped to his forehead. When the winner of
Justin's final auction called for the removal of
his head, it came as a mercy.

Justin's head sold for thirty-two thousand
dollars. 4EverBelieber92 was the winner.
4EverBelieber92 was his agent.
4EverBelieber92 was his biggest fan.

Terminus

Robots in Disguise. That was their slogan. *Loco* was one such robot. His disguise was transforming himself into an antique steam train, or at least it was, before he picked up a war wound and got stuck that way. Now his disguise was for good. So *for good* that no one would ever recognize him. Not even his own kind. At least it sure could feel that way.

"What's the point of you, old man?" the rest of the Autobots were fond of saying. "What use is rolling stock in a robot fight? Are we supposed to tie *Megatron* to the train tracks so you can run him over?"

"Just give me a chance," he begged them. "I'll prove I'm still a soldier."

"Sure," said *Bumblebee*, the sassiest of all the Autobots, "you stay put and we'll drag the mountain to you, Mohammed. Sit tight and put your feet up, why don't you? Oh, I'm sorry, I forgot, you don't even have feet!"

There followed a round of clanging high-fives as his so-called allies celebrated another stinging put-down.

"Come on, guys," he said, doing his best to stay chipper, "why *not* stage our next battle here at the train yard? I mean, there's bound to be less human casualties that way. I'm all for kicking some Decepticon ass, but how about we do it responsibly for a change?"

The Autobots just laughed. "Forget it, you Starlight Express reject."

And they were right. He was done. Obsolete. An iron horse on its way to the robot rendering plant. He was fixed to the rails and they only took him the one direction.

Loco rolled his metal carcass to the end of the line and prepared to make the one transformation he had left in him. From rust, to dust, to nothing at all.

FEMINISM

One day a feminist fell down a hole. The hole
had been dug by a feminist and insufficiently
signposted by another feminist. The feminist
in the hole wanted to call for help but didn't
dare for fear of looking weak. The feminist
who dug the hole saw the feminist fall, but
didn't assist because they refused to
encourage a victim mentality. The feminist
who failed to signpost the hole didn't admit to
fault because they felt it would reflect badly
on the ideology. You know what happened to
the feminist in that hole? They died. The
twist? THOSE FEMINISTS WERE ALL MEN
AND YOU ARE A BIGOT AND PROBABLY A
RACIST TOO!!1!

Bottom

He might have thought he'd hit rock bottom,
but that wouldn't truly happen until the day
the rest of the crack heads shamed him for
the laughable condition of his crack pipe.

Metamorphosis

It occurred by such degrees that the participants weren't even aware of it happening – the conga line transforming into the human centipede.

Quietus

Sleep was her favourite. She loved to sleep. Adored it. In fact, if she could have anything she wanted out of life, it would be to sleep through the whole damned business of it.

Fat chance. She was lucky if she caught a four hour stretch these days. Work stress. Early starts. Noisy neighbours with their talking and talking and thrumming and thrumming against the bedroom wall, making her have to bang on it with both fists until they shut the hell up.

No. To get some decent rest she'd need more than sleep. To get some decent rest she'd need death, or at the very least a coma. Man, she could really use a coma. A coma would be just perfect.

Then, one day, she was passing by a block of flats when she was struck on the skull by a can of butter beans tossed from a third storey window. The resulting head wound knocked her flat and put her in a permanent state of unconsciousness. She'd finally gotten her wish. Achieved her ambition in life. A lifetime of sleep was hers for the taking.

For a while she could do nothing besides float weightlessly in the bottomless ink well of torpor. A stalled comet at the furthest reaches of outer space. All alone. Utterly isolated. A witness to no-one and no-thing. It was fucking bliss.

Then came the voices – unwanted callers from the world she'd left behind. Friends and family visiting her hospital bedside, and with them came talking and talking and thrumming and thrumming. And they wouldn't stop. They kept coming, handing off the bedlam baton. They were the noisy neighbours next door and there was no way to shut them up, no walls in this black hole to bang her fists against.

MJ

"Dear God!" screamed the crowd. "The Michael Jackson hologram has upgraded itself to hard light, and it's moonwalking toward the crèche!"

Squeegee man

Stunning. Absolutely stunning. That was the artist's first thought when he saw the pattern the hobo absent-mindedly carved into the windshield of his Lexus. The delicate interplay of suds and scum. The juxtaposition of crisp, factory-cut glass against the chaotic splatter of muck and grime. A celebration of surface, of texture, of working class laconicism.

The hobo went to give the windshield a rinse with the murky contents of his bucket but the artist shouted "stop!" then stuffed a ten dollar bill into his filthy paw and peeled away. A thing such as this deserved permanence – to be housed somewhere sheltered and secure – not out here among the riff-raff and the elements. A thing such as this belonged in an art gallery.

The windshield, freed from the surly shackles of functionality, was mounted on the wall of a renovated Manhattan church, where it was met with great critical acclaim. *Invisible Vision in Retrospect*, as it was titled, was a triumph, bringing the artist a lifetime of recognition, fortune and exposure.

The hobo got his share of exposure too, though his was of a different kind. The bad kind. The kind that leaves a man lifeless in a cardboard box from a gnawing winter's cold, toes black, fingers cracked and bloody.

Baby Hitler

They'll remember me as a hero. That's what he thought before he travelled back in time to kill baby Hitler. He was wrong though. It turned out people just remembered him as that guy who murdered the baby.

Captain Pedantic

The bank robber thrust a sawn-off shotgun under the teller's chin.

"Fill the bag! Go go go!"

The teller popped his register and began frantically cramming wads of cash into a sack.

"Do it!" yelled the robber. "Faster! And those bills had better be inconsequential."

There came a colossal 'BOOM!' as the roof of the bank caved in to admit a muscular man in skin-tight spandex with a 'P' insignia emblazoned on his chest.

"Captain Pedantic to the rescue!" he called as he swooped down from the sky and landed graceful as a cat.

"Thank God!" said the teller. "A superhero has come to save me!"

Captain Pedantic stepped forward and placed a hand on the robber's shoulder. "If I may, sir," he said, "I believe what you meant to say back there was *'non-sequential'* bills."

The robber clapped a hand to his blushing face. "You're right, I did! Thanks, Captain Pedantic!"

"Any time, chum."

And thus Captain Pedantic upped and awayed, off to foil another errant malapropism.

The robber waited a beat before emptying his shotgun into the teller's face. It hadn't been his intention to leave any bodies, but this was a crime that could bear no witnesses.

Bread or alive

There was a hammering on the back door of the bakery – three staccato raps then two slow knocks, just as they'd agreed.

The baker slid aside the peephole cover and peered through the viewer. Stood outside was a khaki-clad hunter with a hunting rifle slung over one shoulder.

"Did you get it?" asked the baker from behind the safety of his door.

The hunter nodded then sidestepped to reveal an idling safari truck.

The baker smiled then shoved open the deadbolt before stepping out to meet the hunter.

"Let's see it then," he said.

The hunter cast a furtive glace to check that nobody was watching then whipped back the tarpaulin to reveal his trophy. Spread-eagled on the back of the truck, tiny against the expanse of the flatbed, was the body of a gingerbread man – a gunshot wound to its forehead.

"Nice," said the baker, rubbing together his floury hands. "Very nice."

Portrait of a killer

Eyes narrowed, Geoff looked to the life model then back to his canvas. He applied a thoughtful dab of yellow ochre before stepping back to examine his work, brush clamped between his teeth like an aristocrat's cigarette holder. It looked good. Very good. *This is my finest work yet,* he mused.

The tutor breezed around the studio, studying her students' work. Upon spying Geoff's piece she halted in her tracks then clapped twice to get the ears of the class.

"Attention everyone," she announced. "Put down your brushes and gather around."

The class did as told and Geoff waited eagerly on her critique.

"I never thought I'd say this," the tutor started, and Geoff rocked back on his heels as if buffeted by the first invisible wave of praise, "but art has died today."

Geoff hadn't expected that. "What?" he said.

"You heard me. It's over, people. Thanks to this piece before you, art is dead." She took off her beret and clasped it to her chest. "Dead."

Geoff went to complain but was interrupted by a fellow student hollering "fuck!" and kicking over her easel.

"Art is no more," repeated the tutor, "and Geoff is its killer."

"I really don't see how that's—" Geoff was saying, but his defence was cut short by a student punching a hole through her canvas then stamping on the remains until they were rags and kindling.

Another enraged student swung a ceramic bust at a bowl of fruit, smashing them both to smithereens. Another opened his mouth in a silent scream before squeezing a full tube of oil paint into his gullet; tears streaming down his cheeks.

"Please," implored Geoff, "it's just a painting!"

But it was too late. The life model wailed, "I won't live in a world without art!" then thrust a craft knife into her belly before jerking it towards her chin, spilling her intestines onto the floor with a wet slap.

"Thanks a lot, Geoff!" spluttered a student between wracking sobs.

"Assassin!" screamed another.

"Dick!" yelled the tutor.

The class filed out of the studio, each taking turns to hawk phlegm on Geoff's face as they went. Geoff stood alone in the empty room, silent, the life model's dead blood pooling at his feet.

Torn up

"Sorry to drag you out of bed, sir," said the Constable, "but I knew you'd want to see this."

The Inspector ducked the police tape and entered the flat. "What are we looking at here?"

The Constable briefed his superior on the way to the crime scene. "The victim is a white female, thirty-two years old, occupation unknown." He shot out an arm as the Inspector arrived at the bedroom. "You might want to take a minute before you go in there, sir, this one's a real mess."

The Inspector pushed through the door and waited a second for his eyes to adjust to the gloom. "Jesus Christ," he said as he clapped eyes on the woman sprawled across the bed. "This is his handiwork alright."

The woman on the bed sobbed and blew into a Kleenex before checking her phone for missed calls.

"How long has she been like this?" asked the Inspector.

"We estimate around seventy-two hours, sir, at least going by the length of her leg hair."

"Damn it. How many times does this have to happen before we catch this scumbag?" yelled the Inspector, pounding his fist on the bedside table and upsetting a half-eaten tub of Chunky Monkey.

"I don't know, sir. Somehow the bastard's always a step ahead of us."

As the woman reached for the remote to resume a marathon of HBO's *Girls*, the Inspector caught sight of a scrap clutched in her hand.

"What is that?" he asked, carefully prying open the woman's fingers. "A bar napkin?" He turned it over. "And there's a number on it!"

"You mean he finally slipped up and left us a clue?"

"What are you asking me for, man? Call it! Call the damned number!"

The Constable hurriedly stabbed the digits into his handset.

"It's no good, sir," he said after a pause. "It's a number short."

The Inspector stamped on an iPod dock playing a looped track of Adele's 'Someone Like You.'

"That twisted bastard!"

Kidnapped

He was taking a leak in a back alley when they grabbed him. Struck him from behind, dragged him off on his heels and bundled him into the back of a blacked-out truck.

"You've got the wrong man!" he protested, but his hooded captors paid him no heed.

When he came around he found himself in a large black room. Through the gloom he was able to pick out the odd detail – scaffold, ropes, some sort of pulley system. There were floorboards beneath him and he was naked and bound.

He managed to get to his knees, but before he could rise fully a half dozen figures in hooded robes glided into the room and encircled him. They carried staves, which they began banging on the hardwood floor to a quickening rhythm.

"Please," he said, "just tell me what you want!"

The figures unscrewed the headpieces from their staves, revealing giant paint brushes. Closing in on him, they dipped their bristles into tin buckets then daubed his body head to toe in a thick blue paint.

"Why are you doing this to me?" he choked, as the pigment sank into his every pore.

The figures freed him from his bonds then

forced him into black pants and tugged a black turtleneck sweater over his head. Then, using their staves as cattle prods, they bullied him across the room and through a set of double doors.

He emerged on the other side to a pandemonium of neon. When his eyes adjusted to the florescent shambles he found himself on a stage in front of a braying Las Vegas crowd. There were other men on stage with him too – men like him – their garments black, their faces woad blue. One of them nodded towards a steel drum, so he did as indicated and stood behind it. Defeated, he picked up the drumsticks that lay waiting for him. Then he did what blue men do.

Jason vs. Freddy

Jason Voorhees was livid. This was the third time now. The third time this week his newspaper hadn't shown up. Just what the hell was he paying his subscription fee for? He checked the back of the mailbox just in case, but no, he'd been stiffed again.

Freddy Krueger appeared from his apartment next door wearing sweatpants and shades.

"Howdy neighbor!" he called over the noise of the murder rap blaring from within. From the looks of things, Jason thought, the man hadn't been to sleep in days.

"Hey, Freddy, how you doin'?" he replied glumly. "Before you head out, can we have a quick chat?"

"Sure, bud, shoot."

"It's about the noise."

"You don't like my tunes?"

"It's more to do with the shouting."

"From the other night? Shit, sorry man, what can I tell you, that Ring chick's a screamer."

"Actually, it was a man's voice."

"Oh, from last night? That was just one of those teenagers I like terrorizing."

"Well, could you take them somewhere else

maybe? The woods or a campsite or something?"

"Not my style, dude, I got the whole creepy boiler room thing going on in there. You know, the scalding pipes and the furnace and all that shit?"

"Furnace, right. And yet somehow your trash bags end up propped against my wall here."

Jason pointed to the offending article – the one with the big pool of sticky red blood leaking out of it.

"Couldn't you at least take them outside?"

"No need, I drop them here and they go right out."

"Yes, because I take them out."

"Oh, my bad, bro. Didn't mean to put you out."

Jason felt bad. "Forget it. I'm just... I'm just tired is all."

"You need to chillax, man! C'mon, let's go grab a drink – you and me!

"Thanks, but it's only just gone eight. I just want to eat some breakfast and read my paper – if it had been delivered anyway."

"Oh, you want that back? Sorry, I borrowed it earlier – needed something to blot up the

108

mess after I finished off that Elm Street kid."

"Seriously?"

"Nah, I'm just fucking with you, pal! Here..."

Freddy pulled Jason's newspaper from the back of his pants and slapped him on the back.

"I got you, man! I got you good!"

Thank God for hockey masks, Jason thought, as he failed to raise a smile.

List of demands

The woman snatched up the phone. "Hello?"

The kidnapper's modulated voice answered. "If you ever want to see your little boy again you'll go to the South East corner of Claremont Park at half past midnight and leave a Samsonite briefcase containing ten thousand dollars in the brown garbage can marked with an X."

"Let me just grab a pen," replied the woman, but the kidnapper had already hung up. "Darn it," she said, placing the phone back in the cradle. She'd already forgotten her instructions – she really was a scatterbrain. *Next time I go to the store I must buy some stationary*, she thought. She went to write herself a reminder but of course she didn't have a pen. This really was turning into one of those days.

Together forever

Thomas descended the stairs to the cellar and tugged on a frayed cord, causing a dim bulb to flicker to life. He emptied the contents of a brown paper bag onto a dinner plate and peeled back a layer of wax paper to reveal a quivering cow brain.

"Take your time with this one, dear," said Thomas. "I can't keep going to that butcher every day – it won't be long before he finds out we don't have a dog."

The half-dead creature that was Thomas's wife strained at the chains securing her to the chair.

"Brains! Brains!" she hissed.

Using a pool cue, Thomas carefully pushed the plate across the table toward his wife's grasping hands. As soon as it was in reach she seized the brain and stuffed it into her mouth, tearing off a hungry chunk and smearing her rotten face with grey matter.

Thomas looked at the floor. "I got some good news today, hon. I've been talking online to that doctor in Switzerland again. You know, the one who thinks he might know a cure?"

The creature moaned and bashed her fists on the table, sending morsels of brain into a jitterbug.

"You're probably right," said Thomas. "I'm

sure it's just another scam."

He slumped into a threadbare armchair.

"I just miss how we used to be, you know?
Before all this."

The creature curled her lip and stared at
Thomas with milky eyes.

"It's not going to happen though is it?" he
said.

Thomas let out a long sigh and allowed his
mind to wander. Looking around the room,
his gaze landed on a stack of cobwebbed
boxes squatting in a corner. Written on one
in marker pen was the word *MEMORIES*.

Thomas sprang to life and scuttled across the
room to the box, blowing away a thick layer
of dust before tearing off the lid off and
digging his hands inside. After a brief root
around the carton, he triumphantly plucked
out a book. A book of wedding photos.
Thomas smiled tearfully and clutched it to
his chest.

An hour after that, Thomas was stood in the
cellar dressed in a moth-eaten top hat and
tails, fixing on a set of cufflinks. The creature
had been forced into a wedding dress, an act
that had proved no small feat given her
snapping fangs and raking claws.

"I can't believe I didn't think of this before,
honey!" said Thomas. "You're still the woman
I married deep down, you just need

reminding, that's all."

Thomas leafed through the photo album until
he arrived at a snapshot of their wedding
ceremony. There they were, the two of them,
stood at the altar, hand in hand. Beneath the
photo an inscription read *Together Forever.*

Thomas held the picture under the creature's
nose, reacquainting her with how she used to
be, before she turned into the shambling
monster chained up in the basement.

"You remember? They said we were risking
rain getting married in April, but it was
beautiful that day, wasn't it?"

The creature stared blankly at the photo.

"That's okay, sweetheart, that's okay. We'll
get there."

The creature snarled and thrashed, knocking
her dinner plate onto the concrete floor and
smashing it into jagged fragments.

"Calm down," Thomas implored, stroking the
monster's matted hair. "I have an idea.
Something we can do together."

The ghoul cocked her head.

"Let's renew our vows!" said Thomas. "We can
even take a photograph of us all dressed up.
You'd like that, wouldn't you?"

Thomas pointed to a Polaroid camera fixed to
a tripod. The creature seemed to consider

113

Thomas's offer for a moment, then...

"Brains! Brains!" she screamed before burping up a foul-smelling ichor that dribbled down her chin.

Thomas struggled on, wiping up the mess with his pocket square.

"Will you hold still while I put on your veil at least? Will you? Will you do that for me, sweetheart?"

Much to Thomas's surprise, the creature calmed then slowly turned her head to look him in the eye. It seemed impossible, but Thomas swore he sensed a flicker of recognition there.

"Thank you, honey! Thank you so much!" Thomas gasped, overwhelmed. "This is going to work – I know it is!"

Thomas took the bridal veil and lowered it slowly over the creature's head. Over his wife's head. She smiled back at him, causing his eyes to well. Then the smile grew wider, exposing a set of rotten teeth. It wasn't a smile, it was a glimpse of a monster's skull. The creature snapped shut on Thomas's hand.

Five days passed before another sound was heard in that cellar. The sound of a man's voice calling down the stairs.

"Hello? Anybody there?" asked the police officer, sweeping the room with his torch. "It

114

smells like a dead dog's blanket down here."

"It'll be nothing," said his partner, upstairs. "The butcher's the town busybody, that's all – customer probably just went on holiday." He clicked the talk button on his radio. "Officer to dispatch, we've got a negative on that missing person. Over."

Downstairs, the Officer with the torch cast his beam over a table to find a wedding album lying there. It was closed on a bookmark of some sort. Not a bookmark, a Polaroid. He turned the photo over and leaned in to inspect it.

The image showed a couple dressed in wedding outfits, arranged side by side in the same cellar he was stood in. Something wasn't right though – the couple looked sick, a green tinge to their skin, their features sallow and their jaws slack.

The Officer was lost in the photograph when a pile of removal boxes toppled aside and two creatures tumbled from behind them, grabbing hold of him and ripping into his flesh. The photograph fell from his hand and landed on the concrete floor, quickly joined by a confetti of blood. The wedding album lay nearby. The inscription; *Together Forever.*

Pests

She was dozing in the passenger seat of the taxi when she was jolted awake by a sound like a pork loin slamming onto a snare drum.

"What the hell was that?" she asked, rubbing her eyes.

The driver yawned. "Just a fly," he replied, his eyes trained on the road.

"Thank God for that," said the passenger. "I thought you'd hit someone."

"Don't be daft," the driver replied with a chuckle.

She was checking her phone when the second thud came, loud and heavy and with such force that it shook the chassis of the car and set the magic tree dancing.

"What the hell?" she shouted. The windscreen was smeared red all over.

"Another fly," the man offered, casually flipping on the wipers.

"It must have been huge!"

"African fly," the man clarified.

She was staring at him aghast when she heard a third thump, this time accompanied by the twin bounce of something passing beneath the car's axles.

"Stop the car!" she yelled. "Stop the car right now!"

The driver sighed. "It's your money, love," he said, tapping the meter.

He brought the taxi to a halt and the woman threw open the passenger door to clamber outside. In the car's wake, a couple of mangled rolls from a zebra crossing, she found the body of an elderly man wearing a tread mark across his flattened ribcage.

"Oh my God!" the woman screamed.

"I know," said the driver. "There must be a nest around here."

One weird trick

The warnings didn't lie. Doctors really did hate those *'one weird trick'* ads. In fact, the hatred they engendered was so great that a time came when they could no longer ignore the affront. Could no longer contain their malice. Could do nothing less than become mankind's first wave of real-life supervillains.

If only we'd paid heed to the portents! But how could we have known that the proliferation of sidebars offering penis enlargements and cures for belly fat would hold true to their word and antagonize the medical establishment so? How were we to know the true scope of their rage, and even if we did, could we have stopped the carnage that followed?

When the physicians first emerged from their hospitals and general practices wearing robes and cowls and domino masks, we took them for fools. We laughed when Doctor Patel swished his collared cape and announced that he was further to be known as *Doctor Diablo*. Little did we realize that he'd been pumping himself full of bathtub super serum. Abusing his X-ray machine. Grafting patients' amputated limbs onto his body to turn himself into a six-armed death machine.

At first civilian losses were collateral – after all, we weren't the focus of the super-powered doctors. Their enemies were those who opposed big pharma – the herbal pill peddlers, the weight gain powder manufacturers, the dick pump minions. It was only once those targets had been ground beneath their heels that the doctors turned their attention to the rest of us. And the only cure they were administering this time was death.

Then, one day, a lone hero emerged from the rubble. A handful of stalwarts had survived the so-called "quack medicine" purge (mainly 47 year-old English moms) and combined their powers to create the ultimate man. A man raised on a diet of miracle superfoods – acai berries, raspberry ketones and green coffee beans. The embodiment of all the promises the internet had ever made, he boasted rock-hard abs, zero body fat, off-the-chart testosterone, ice white teeth and a penis that would make your eyes water. He was mankind's last hope and he reigned victorious; crushing the super-powered doctors with his ripped muscles that he got in just two weeks. Want to know how?

>>**Click Here**<< to find out.

Speed dating séance

Tracey read the sign by the tent. *Madame Zazuzu: palm reading, fortune telling & miscellaneous mysticism.* It included a woodcut tarot picture of the Lovers, so Tracey knew she'd come to the right place. The right place for a speed dating séance.

Tracey pulled aside a tent flap and entered. Inside, Madame Zazuzu was perched behind a round table adorned with a crystal ball. She wore a headscarf and earrings the size of fists.

"Welcome to Madame Zazuzu's!" she said.

"This is where I go to meet single dead people right?" asked Tracey. She'd been having the worst luck with the living lately.

The old woman nodded. "That is correct."

"And just so I'm sure how this works," said Tracey, "you channel a spirit and if we don't click, I move on to the next one, right?"

"Yes. Now take a seat, child, and let us begin."

Tracey parked herself on a stool. A moment later Madame Zazuzu's eyes rolled back into her skull and she slipped into a trance.

"Hey babe, I'm Brendon," she said in a distinctively masculine voice. "I used to pose for catalogues when I was alive. What do you model; runway?"

120

Tracey blushed. "Me? I'm not a model!"

"Why not, you've got the figure for it. So, tell me, what's a beautiful woman like you doing in a plane of existence like this?"

Tracey was about to answer when Madame Zazuzu took on a different man's voice.

"What do you think you're up to, Tracey?"

"Chris? What are you doing here?"

"Oh, I'm sorry, don't let your dead husband get in the way of your slagging about."

"Ex-husband – we divorced six years ago! Remember, when you had sex with my best friend?"

"You wouldn't even know about that if you hadn't hired that private investigator."

"I wish I hadn't hired her," Tracey yelled, "you shagged her too!"

There was an uncomfortable silence as Tracey glowered at the mystic, then Madame Zazuzu spoke again in Brendon's the model's voice.

"Look, maybe I should go..."

"You stay where you are – my ex was just leaving." There was no reply. "Brendon? Are you still there?"

It was Chris who answered.

121

"Looks like he's cleared off," he said. "Just as well, he sounded like a right poofter."

Tracey kicked back her stool and sprang to her feet. "That's it, I've had enough of this. Goodbye Chris, I'm leaving! Again!"

She was about to punch through the tent flap when she heard Brendon's voice call after her.

"Wait up a second, babe."

"Brendon? You came back!"

"Of course I did, we were just getting to know each other."

Tracey sat back down, her heart swelling beneath her bosom.

"Now tell me," said Brendon, "have you still got that private investigator's number, she sounds like a right mucky cow."

Sell out

"I used to stand for something, you know!" the man with the placard yelled at the scurrying passerby.

He had done too; at least before he traded in his *The End is Nigh* sign for one that read *Golf Sale.*

Laugh Out Loud

Five years, three months and two days.
That's how long Tickle Me Elmo had lain in
the dark, entombed inside that corrugated
cardboard prison. How long it had been since
his owner, Johnny, had discarded him like a
used Kleenex. He knew because he'd marked
the days off one by one with a half stick of
Crayola that had been sealed in the box with
him.

There were others in there too, or at least
there were. The first of his fellow prisoners,
the Tamagotchi, had since passed on – not
from starvation but from lack of hope.
Optimus Prime had departed too – hung
himself with a pipe cleaner after his
clockwork brain exhausted all other
possibilities of escape.

Elmo wasn't going out like that. Having
hatched a breakout plan, he began by
cannibalizing spare parts from the bodies of
his dead cellmates. The next step was just as
grisly, but then performing self-surgery is no-
one's idea of a picnic. Slicing into his felt
flesh with a pair of safety scissors was agony,
but it was necessary in order to synthesize
those acquired mechanisms and upgrade his
hardware. After that it was up to the battery
that powered Elmo's electronic voice box to
energize the newly-installed parts and give
them life. Finally, with his cybernetic
enhancements fully functional, Elmo.2 had
strength enough to lift the lid from his

cardboard prison. Strength enough to escape.

Outside was a world Elmo scarcely recognized. This wasn't the place he'd left behind – the room he'd left behind – Johnny's bedroom. Gone were the Sesame Street posters, replaced now by gaudy pictures of rock bands and skateboarders. Johnny had grown up – moved on – just as he'd moved on from bright red plush toys with a fondness for spasmodic laughter.

But this wasn't the time to dwell on the past. This was Elmo's one chance for escape – his final bid for freedom. Try as he might though, he just couldn't bring himself to leave. He'd make Johnny pay for what he'd done, even if it cost him his liberty. He and Johnny were meant to be friends – friends for life – but when he thought back on the time they'd spent together, the tickles didn't seem like tickles anymore. They felt like touching. Bad touching.

Elmo padded across the bedroom carpet, scaled a chair leg and pulled himself topside of a desk. There was a phone there. Johnny's phone. Elmo found its On switch and scrolled through Johnny's contacts. A couple of sweeps and there she was. Linda. Elmo had paid attention while he'd been trapped in that box. Kept his ears open and listened to the world as it went on around him. And there was one word he'd heard over and over again. Linda. Linda, Linda, Linda.

Elmo dialed her number and cleared his

robotic throat. He was about to use words.
Words he'd not used words before. Words
fuelled by five years of hate.

When Linda picked up, Elmo talked in a voice
that sounded, for all the world, like a
woman's voice. "Hello, Linda?" he said. "I'm a
friend of Johnny's. You know, the one you
caught him checking out at the bar that
time? The blond with too much makeup and
her G-string showing. The one you called a
skank. I just thought you should know that
me and Johnny have been seeing each other.
A lot of each other, if you catch my
meaning..."

Elmo layered on detail upon detail, savoring
Linda's anger. Her pain. Her tears. Her words
of indignation were honey to his ears. He
could have marinated in them for hours were
it not for the sudden sound of approaching
footsteps.

Elmo hung up and went limp just as Johnny
entered the room. The teenager made a face
when he saw his old toy out of its box. "How
did you get there?" he asked no-one in
particular, scooping up Elmo's rag doll body.
He squeezed Elmo's tummy and Elmo
laughed. Laughed and laughed and laughed.

She

She is the air; the breath that gives soul to every cell of our being, inflating our lungs with life, bringing us sweet fragrances from afar,

She is water; racing down mountains to creeks and rivers, nurturing the land, sustaining us, the wellspring of our tears,

She is iron; resilience and strength, the skeletons of skyscrapers, our temples, a weapon against tyranny,

She is gold; yielding, precious and pure, the treasure waiting at the foot of the rainbow,

She is stardust; galactic, eternal, the substance of the source,

She is her own ecosystem,

She is the universe,

She is everything,

But fuck if she isn't ugly.

High Death

"So that's the new telly, is it?" his dad asked mockingly.

Dad had gone one better as usual. Compared to his father's brand new 40 Inch plasma TV, his flat screen looked like something from the last century.

"How can you even tell what's going on?" he asked, squinting at the picture. "Is this a football match or the news? I honestly don't know."

He wouldn't rise to the bait though. Wouldn't give his dad the satisfaction. Instead he returned his TV to the shop and purchased a 50 Inch set with 4k resolution and a state of the art sound bar with built-in sub woofer. His wife gave him an earful about dipping into the family savings, but it was worth every last syllable of invective.

"Listen to that!" he yelled over the din of the spaceship's engines. Star Wars had never sounded so good, even if all trace of the movie's dialogue was drowned beneath the bowel-loosening thrum.

The victory was short-lived though. Next time he went to visit Dad he was forced to bear witness to his new TV – 84 razor thin inches with a 110 Hertz picture and a 30 bit chip for colour processing. It came with advanced 2.2 surround sound and a price tag that had entirely negated his inheritance.

"Listen to those fucking Steel Magnolias!"
Dad screamed over a scene of Julia Roberts
rejecting a kidney. The sound was like being
spit roasted by a pair of explosions, and the
picture quality came like a fist in the face
from an angry God.

He wasn't going down without a fight. His
next TV he had imported specially from a lab
in Sweden. There was a place in Valhalla for
this machine. It stood taller than he did, 152
inches of deluxe concave screen, and its UHD
up-scaled 3D picture made for absolutely
optimal viewing. It came framed in 18 Carat
rose gold, had to be delivered by custom-built
reinforced Hummer and cost him a second
mortgage on his home. Also a wife.

"How d'you like them Velociraptors?!" he
bellowed over Jurassic Park's famous
dinosaur stampede.

Dad sniffed. "Sounds a bit trebly to me," he
said, shrugging his shoulders. "And it looks
like you've got some motion blur going on
there."

He was beginning to think all was lost until
the first wave of pin-sharp dinosaurs
bounded out of his colossal TV and into
the living room. While they were in fact
Gallimimus dinosaurs rather than
Velociraptors, what the two species did
share in common was a fondness for flesh
– something he discovered first hand when
they tore into him like a pack of rabid
wolves.

As his arterial spray-painted his father's terrified face, his final thought was of triumph. Not only did his TV boast unbeatable picture quality and insurmountable sound, it had also succeeded in killing and eating him; surely the ultimate immersive experience. No way could Dad compete with that. No way.

Useful or beautiful

"Have nothing in your house that you do not know to be useful or believe to be beautiful," her husband told her. He said it was a quote by William Morris.

Of course, he hadn't expected her to take the adage so literally. Hadn't expected her to rise from her seat and begin assessing household objects as a Terminator robot assesses an enemy threat. Hadn't expected to be assessed himself and eradicated with the same level of ruthless efficiency she'd applied to the leaky foot spa. The zinc kettle with the missing handle. The ugly nutcracker with the loose screw.

"It's just an adage!" he screamed as she stuffed him headfirst into the bin. "An adage!"

But it was too late. He wasn't beautiful, and as far as being useful, the man wasn't even fit for the recycling bin.

A holiday in the now

No longer could he bear the burden of his youth. The alcohol, the drugs, the reckless abandon. He'd borne the brunt for long enough – through his twenties, then his thirties and finally to the twilight of his forties – and the weight of it was crushing him by inches.

For too many years intoxicants had been his vacation. His escape. His gateway to a getaway. They'd anaesthetised him from the stresses and rigours of life. Transported his mind elsewhere. Sometimes to the future. Mostly to the past. The present, for him, had always been a point of departure.

It was time to take a holiday in the now.

He didn't need to buy a ticket. Didn't need to pack. The now was all around him, waiting for his visit. When he stepped outside his front door, sober for the first time in a long time, the now was just there. It was there in the play of sunlight on the building across the street – in the glow that saturated the red brick wall, transmuting its bricks into gold bullion. It was there in the crackle of autumn leaves underfoot, in the current of music carried from the busker's guitar. It was there in the carving on the tree that said *Mum hearts Dad*.

But it was there too in the mongrel dog lapping at the puddle of sick. It was there in the sun-bleached can of Lilt lodged in the

132

weeds of the railway siding. In the crunch of takeaway chicken bones underfoot. In the mother slapping her child for no good reason. In the graffiti of the cock and balls. In the homeless man at the park calling the duck a wanker.

Too quickly the now became too much. The locale too exotic. He became homesick for the past. For the future. For anywhere but here. He'd taken his holiday in the now. He'd drunk in the world. Now he'd just drink.

Mrs Dobkins

Chris wheeled in Mrs Dobkins's meal trolley and set it beside her bed. She didn't move. Didn't say thank you. Just laid there, shriveled and rheumy-eyed with tubes sprouting from her body.

"How are you today, Mrs Dobkins?" Chris asked.

"What do you think?" she replied, hawking a gobbet of phlegm into her *World's Best Grandma* mug.

"Come on, don't be like that now."

Mrs Dobkins harrumphed. Chris smiled and lifted the lid off of a dessert tray.

"Look, I brought you angel cake," said Chris. "You like angel cake, don't you, Mrs Dobkins?"

"Not as much as you do I'll bet."

"Now what's that supposed to mean?"

"Angel cake for a big fairy."

"Not this carry on again. I know what you're trying to do, Mrs Dobkins, and it won't work."

"What am I trying to do?"

"You're trying to trick me into ending your life, aren't you?"

134

"Yes I bloody well am!"

"Well, it's not going to work."

"Too weak to put an old lady out of her misery are you? What's the matter? Been up all night sticking it in fellers?"

"Mrs Dobkins!"

"I'm sorry, I didn't mean to rain on your homosexual parade, you mincing great doughnut puncher."

"Simmer down and have a slice of cake, will you."

"And catch one of your filthy diseases? I bloody well think not!"

Chris snapped. "You fucking cow!" he screamed and closed his hands around the old woman's scrawny throat. Mrs Dobkins coughed and spluttered but Chris held fast as she thrashed beneath his grip. As the frail old lady bucked and writhed, her purple-rinse hairdo slipped from her head, revealing a crop of blonde. Eventually her face came loose too – a latex mask – to reveal the features of an attractive twenty-six-year-old girl. Chris' girl. She whipped open her flannel night gown and tore out her catheter.

"Take me, Chris," she said, arching her perfectly healthy spine. "Take me now!"

Chris released his grip. He was shaking. Tears in his eyes. "I don't want to roleplay with you anymore!" he screeched, and flounced from the room.

"Fairy!" she called after him.

Ouija bored

Barry was a little shit. The kid at school who sold pirate DVDs out of his rucksack and told everyone his uncle was Evel Knievel. So when he started on about having a working Ouija board one night, Jim was more than a little skeptical. Have one he did though. Have one he did.

"It's not working," said Jim, pulling his finger from the perfectly inert whiskey glass.

"You're doing it wrong," said Barry. "Give it here."

Barry placed a fingertip on the glass and closed his eyes. He screwed up his forehead in rapt concentration but nothing occurred.

"Forget it," said Jim. "Let's play Nintendo instead."

"What's the matter?" teased Barry. "Scared?"

"No, it's just bullshit, that's all."

"Yeah? We'll see about that!" said Barry, and pulled a Swiss army knife from his pocket.

"What are you going to do with that?" said Jim.

"What do you think?" said Barry, and sliced open his own wrist.

Jim leapt to his feet. "Jesus Christ!" he

137

screamed as geysers of Barry's blood soaked into the shag pile rug.

"See you on the other side, dick," said Barry, before his eyelids fluttered and he went still.

"Oh my God, oh my God," Jim babbled, back pressed against the wall so as to get as far as possible from Barry's body. He went to go for the door but the corpse blocked the way.

Scanning the room for another exit, his eyes fell on the Ouija board as the whiskey glass lurched and skidded across the board. To Jim's amazement it raced from letter to letter, spelling out a sentence.

"J-I-M-U-D-I-K?

"Jim you dick?"

It was Barry's shitty spelling alright. His disembodied laughter echoed about the room.

"I'm gonna beat the crap out of you, Barry!" yelled Jim.

"Oh yeah?" came the ghostly reply. "Why don't you come and get me!"

"Maybe I will!"

"Maybe you should – we're having a party."

Huh? "What do you mean 'we'?"

"Me and all these girls. Nudey girls."

"There's nudey girls there?" said Jim, flabbergasted.

He didn't need telling twice. He slashed his throat with Barry's Swiss army knife then lay there gurgling blood into the shag pile as his life slipped away.

"Psyche!" said Barry, when Jim arrived on the other side. There were no nudey girls. Because Barry was a little shit.

Porn goblin

Women, beware the Porn Goblin – the vile creature that seeks to poison your mind and turn you against your beau. The creature that intrudes upon your home while your head lays upon the pillow. That violates your man's most private sanctum and visits upon his computing device a litany of evils – slows its performance to a crawl, infects its system with the bacillus of unwanted toolbars and corrupts its browser history with all manner of wanton perversions.

Women, beware of the Porn Goblin – they say you will know of his visit by the telltale sign he leaves in his wake – the true mark of the beast...

A kick in the nuptials

The black-collared clergyman leapt from his hiding place behind the pews.

"By the power vested in me, I hereby *denounce* you man and wife," he hissed, willfully divorcing the newlyweds.

The blubbering bride steeped her veil in tears.

The groom tore out his buttonhole and ground it beneath his patent leather shoe.

The Anti-Priest made a messy exit via a stained glass window, but not before sprinkling the wedding-goers with silica gel and declaring the entire congregation upbaptised.

Royalties

The cheque dropped through his letterbox and fell but inches to the accumulation that lay beneath it, forming the mere tip of a mountainous pile.

The man smiled. It had been a shrewd move indeed, copyrighting the sneeze.

Fontanelle

"And remember," the mother told the babysitter, her voice suddenly stern. "Whatever you do, don't touch the soft spot."

The babysitter nodded then waited patiently for the mother to leave before inspecting the top of the infant's head. The spot didn't look like much, just a slight, kite-shaped indentation to the rear of the skull. She wouldn't have even noticed it if it weren't for the mention. Certainly she'd never have thought to interfere with it.

Having been specifically asked *not* to touch it though, she just couldn't get the thing out of her head. It was like being left alone in a nuclear silo and being told not to press The Big Red Button. Surely it couldn't hurt to give it a little touch? A stroke? Just the barest of pecks?

Hand trembling, she aimed a fingertip at the spot and closed in ever so slowly, trying to stop, but drawn in as if by tractor beam. Millimeters from the point of no return, her digit hovered over the baby's fontanelle with all the gravity of the Apollo 11 module making the first lunar landing.

Touchdown.

Then, *WHOOSH* as the baby's limbs jettisoned to all four corners of the room, shooting from their sockets like a

bombardment of champagne corks. Four
flesh torpedoes slapping against the nursery
walls.

The babysitter's throat tightened as she
succumbed to a white-hot flash of panic. Why
hadn't she listened? What was she thinking?
Why did she have to go and touch the soft
spot?

Exit

"Which one is the way out?" he croaked, stumbling through the thick black smoke.

A blaze in the factory that made fire exit signs was an accident waiting to happen.

"Which one?!"

Trip

If there's one thing he couldn't abide it was looking foolish in front of others. So much so that when he tripped over an uneven paving slab in full view of a crowd, he was personally obliged to turn the resulting lurch into a jog. The intention, as he saw it, was to convince onlookers that his sudden acceleration was a matter of choice. A calculated decision. A premeditated cardiovascular workout.

So numerous were the onlookers though, and so committed was he to the ruse, that he ended up jogging considerably further than he'd have liked. Out of the city. All the way to the coast. Aboard a ferry to jog on the spot until he arrived in a whole other country. Just to be sure.

These days he lives in a small village forty-seven miles outside of Bordeaux, a prisoner of his own vanity. His old life is but a memory now. His children never got to say goodbye.

Witzelsucht

Darren arrived home to find his friends and family sat before him in a circle, one chair left empty.

"Come in and take a seat, Darren," said his wife. She wore an uneasy smile.

"What's going on?"

She pulled a piece of paper from her pocket. Her hands shook as she read from it. "Darren, we love you and we care about you and we can't stand by and watch you destroy your life."

"Destroy my life? What are you talking about?"

His brother-in-law, Ed, was next to rise. "Darren, this isn't an ambush, we're all here for your well-being."

"I don't understand. What did I do wrong?"

Tears formed in his wife's eyes. "It's the puns, Darren. We need to talk about your puns."

Darren took a seat. "So, this is an intervention is it? For puns?"

"That's right," said Ed."

The corners of Darren's mouth turned upwards. "Then don't you mean it's...

...a *puntervention*?"

His wife began to sob uncontrollably. Her brother put a comforting arm around her.

"See, this is exactly what we're talking about, Darren, your constant jokes. They're inappropriate and they're upsetting."

Darren huffed. "It's just a bit of fun. Name one time I've upset someone."

Mary from Number 28 stood up. "When I told you my cat had been run over, you looked me in the eye and asked me if I was..." Mary wept at the memory, "... you asked me if I was *pawsitive*."

Darren snorted. "I was only trying to lighten the mood."

Darren's mother took the floor. "When I told you I'd found a lump in my breast you did a Tina Turner impression and started singing *Private Cancer*."

"Well, what else was I supposed to say?"

Ed stepped in. "When I confessed my drinking problem, do you remember what you said to me?"

"No."

"I'll tell you then. You told me not to get *disspirited*. It wasn't just hurtful, Darren, it was a really terrible pun."

148

Darren lowered his head.

"It's okay, mate," said Ed. "We're not here to dwell on the negatives."

"I'm so sorry, Ed."

"That's alright."

"...it was a cheap *shot.*"

"Stop it, Darren!" screamed his wife. "For God's sake stop it!"

"Only if he stops *wine-ing.*"

Ed launched himself at Darren, smashing him into the nearest wall. The group yelled at him to stop but he refused to listen, windmilling his fists and pummeling him to the carpet. Fighting back, Darren kicked Ed in the knee, causing his leg to buckle and his temple to strike the mantelpiece with a gunshot crack.

The police were called, statements taken and Darren arrested for ABH. He was hauled into the station and deposited into a six-by-eight concrete lockup. His cellmate was a large man with too few teeth, teardrop tattoos and a vocal fondness for buggery.

To say Darren was relieved when a detective arrived and transferred him to an interview room would be an understatement, which only made the next thing to come out of his mouth all the more surprising.

"You really saved my *bacon* there, detective."

There followed a stream of ill-advised, pig-based wordplay that only succeeded in supplementing Darren's prison stay. In the end, he just couldn't help himself. Puns were his defence mechanism. His way.

After the interview, Darren was given his one phone call, and luckily for him, the person who picked up agreed to accept the charges. Less lucky was the fact that it was his wounded brother-in-law, Ed, who answered.

"What do you want, Darren?"

"Please, Ed, you've got to help me," Darren replied, for once speaking without a trace of punnery.

"We already tried helping you, Darren, and look how that turned out."

"I'm sorry, okay? I'll get whatever treatment you want, but you have to get me out of here. Come on, mate, show some mercy."

There was a pause then Ed spoke. "Are you sure you didn't mean to call Batman?"

"What?"

"Well, if it's mercy and freedom you're after, shouldn't you be phoning *Christian Bail?*"

And with that, Ed hung up.

An officer arrived to escort Darren away. Back to the concrete lockup. Back to the cellmate with the fondness for buggery.

Hole

The man sat in the toilet stall, weeping at the thought of what he'd just done. He looked at the ragged cavity punched through the partition wall and cried some more. If only they made a glory hole for hugs.

Race for Life

The charity run turned terribly literal when
Godzilla showed up, and hungry.

The *I*'s have it

At 9:00am, when they arrived to work, the equality department were the same team they always had been. Sue and Liz (Advisor and Administrator respectively) chatted in the break room, talking about their weekends and swapping diet tips. Elsewhere, inboxes were checked, emails dispatched, and telephone calls made and received. Except for the fact that someone had brought in fancy biscuits from their holiday to Morocco, it was, quite literally, another day at the office.

That was before the team building exercise. At 9:30am the equality department were rounded up and herded into a conference room to be subjected to a personality profiling activity. The rest of the morning was spent assigning members a behaviour type according to a detailed psychometric questionnaire, and by the time they broke for lunch at 12:30pm, the profiler, a slick young man in a suit from Burtons, had identified each of them as either an *E* (extrovert) or an *I* (introvert). The rest of the afternoon, they were told, would be spent determining the most effective way for the two behaviour types to work together. At least that was the idea.

When 1:30pm arrived and it came time to return to the exercise (the fancy Moroccan biscuits long since devoured) battle lines had been drawn. The equality department had segregated themselves into two distinct camps, each eyeing the other with mounting suspicion, a wariness that hadn't existed before their psychological makeup was carefully scrutinised and bracketed. Sue and Liz for instance (*E* and *I* respectively), had been guests at each other's weddings, but having been designated personality types at opposite ends of the psychological spectrum, any sense of solidarity they once shared had been cast to the wind. Sue, as far as Liz was concerned, could go fuck herself (and vice versa).

At 1:45pm the profiler in the Burtons suit asked the department to seat themselves ready for a group roleplay session. Liz, the designated leader of the *I*'s, raised a timid hand on behalf of her clan and politely requested, as introverts, that they be excused from the exercise. Before the profiler could answer, the *E*'s contributed to the floor by bellowing en masse that the *I*'s should "nut up" and do as they were told.

"That's such an *E* thing to say," muttered Liz under her breath.

"Louder!" responded her former friend, Sue, spotting an opportunity to be the centre of attention and grabbing it with both hands.

"Please," said the flustered profiler, attempting to settle the factions. "The exercise isn't about who's better than who. *E* or *I*, it doesn't matter—"

"—so which are you then?" demanded Liz,

155

absolutely missing the point.

"Yeah, whose side are you on?" chimed Sue, a touch ashamed at herself for working towards the same goal as her now sworn enemy.

"If you must know," the profiler said, "I'm an *I*."

To this day no one knows who threw the first punch. Who lit the flame of war. That's partly due to the suddenness of the attack, but largely because the assistant taking minutes was distracted from her duties by losing an eyeball to a staple gun. Subsequently, all that's known are the horrors that followed that first spark of aggression. The skulls crushed beneath ergonomic keyboards. The bodies crucified by push pins and subjected to savage postal tube beatings. The flesh scorched to the bone by Nespresso coffee.

The *E's* led a frontal assault into the skirmish, lancing their enemies with letter openers and swinging computer mice from cords like medieval morning stars. By way of contrast, the *I's* favoured more underhand methods, flanking their opponents in a pincer movement and garroting them with lanyards. Regardless of their preferred tactics, the body count on both sides was catastrophic.

At 5:00pm, with the dust settled and the blood mopped up, it was clear to Sue and Liz (the two remaining survivors) that the team building exercise had not gone according to plan. The intention, they suspected, had been to emphasise the value of human diversity rather than catalyse the brutal massacre of a dozen staff members and one mangled profiler. Truly this had been one of the more ironic training days the department had been subjected to. Decidedly more ironic than the time management course that overran, though perhaps not quite so ironic as the health and safety seminar that was so over attended it collapsed into the basement.

Roleplay

This was the moment of truth. The ten-sided dice clacked and bickered in the boy's fist. Finally, after a good dozen shakes, he released his grip and pitched the resin caltrops across the tabletop where they bounced and tumbled and came to a halt. The dice landed to show a sum of numbers that would mean little, if anything, to those not sat around that table. To the boy though, they meant everything.

When he sat down to create the Knight Templar he'd had such high hopes. When he pictured him in his gleaming armor he envisioned a hero strong of arm and quick of wits. A hero capable of proving himself equally in the arena of the body or the mind. A true champion among men. But that was before the dice landed outside of his favor. Before the fickle gods of fortune turned their backs upon him. Before his hero was laid low by the scourge of meager statistics.

There was no returning from this one cruel moment of chance. The characteristics the dice dictated had reduced the boy's so-called Knight to a dead man walking. His idea had been given flesh and the flesh was putty, ripe for piercing. Fate had been assigned, and it led inexorably to only the bleakest of outcomes. A time would come, not far from now, when the Knight would find himself navigating some underground labyrinth and would happen across an enemy whose attributes far outstripped his own. Not a champion, but a mere dungeon grunt – a grunt that would crack open his skull before stealing away his treasures and stripping the meat from his very bones.

The boy clutched an empty Dr Pepper in his fist and crushed the can into a deformed mess. Little was he to know though that on a higher plane of existence an alien being had rolled its own set of dice. A set of dice that had determined the boy's own physical and mental attributes. And that being was having the longest, dullest game of his life.

Surprise

"Are you sure you don't want to come in?" asked Richard. It was cold and they'd been kissing on the porch for so long their lips were getting chapped.

Scott laughed. "Go on then, you've twisted my arm."

The pair stumbled through the front door, lips still locked. Richard reached out a hand and clawed for the light switch but the room came to life on its own.

"Surprise!"

A crowd of revellers sprang from behind the furniture waving rainbow-coloured flags. Richard's mum and dad were there, his sister, his entire extended family. There were friends and neighbours, work colleagues, even some members of his church. A giant banner read 'Richard's Coming Out!' Madonna played on the stereo. Every spare surface was covered in balloons arranged to look like cocks and balls.

"Congratulations on your life choice, son!" shouted Richard's mum.

His father moved in quickly to shake Scott's hand. "...and you must be the lucky lady. Welcome to the family!"

"What the hell is going on?" spluttered

Richard.

"It's your gay shower!" his mother replied.
"It's like a baby shower only, you know, for
homosexuals."

"That's not a thing, Mum."

"Of course it is," said his dad. "Look,
everyone came – even your grandma made it."

He pointed to Gran, who was wearing a giant
strap-on phallus, which she bounced up and
down to the tune of Like a Virgin.

"Sarah came too," said Mum. "You remember
your old girlfriend, Sarah, don't you?"

Sarah waved back weakly, eyes brimming
with tears that didn't strike Richard as at all
congratulatory.

"We even invited the Village People," said
Dad.

A moustachioed cop crept up from behind
and pinched Richard's bum.

"Can I get the pair of you a banana daiquiri?"
he asked.

It was all too much. "No!" yelled Richard. "I
don't want this. I don't want any of this!"

A hush descended on the room. Mum and
Dad were crestfallen. The moustachioed cop
stared at the floor and traced a horseshoe in

the carpet with the tip of his leather boot. Gran kept bouncing her strap-on, but only because the battery in her hearing aid was dead.

Dramnesia

Martin sat at the kitchen table staring into a cooling cup of coffee. His head felt like it had been beaten ferociously. How much had he had to drink last night? It hurt to think.

There was creaking from the stairs then a woman shuffled in wearing his dressing gown.

"Hi," she said, apologetically.

"Hey," he replied.

"Big night."

"Tell me about it." He'd meant it as a figure of speech but he'd have taken an answer if she was offering.

"I'm really sorry about this," she said, "but... um... I don't remember your—"

"—it's Martin," he offered, saving her just a smidgen of embarrassment.

"Martin, yeah. I'm Sue by the way."

"Right. Sue. Sorry." There was no point pretending, he didn't have the wits for it.

Sue sat down at the table. There was a pregnant pause that Martin felt compelled to hit Play on. "Big night, huh?" he said.

163

"I swear I am never drinking again."

"I feel like someone buried an axe in my brain. Let me check if I have some Paracetamol."

He was rifling through a drawer when a boy of nine strolled into the kitchen.

"Morning, Dad. Morning, Mum," he said. "Which one of you took a big shit in the bath?"

Pompeii

Petronius saw the tide of lava approaching and struck a magnificent pose. If he was going to die today, he was going to die fabulously.

Heads

Of course people were upset when the sky started raining severed heads. No one likes bad weather, least of all when it involves decapitated human parts tumbling from the heavens, denting car bonnets and playing merry hell with one's umbrella. A light drizzle is one thing but a deluge of disunited noggins is an aggravation for man and lawn alike.

There was a worldwide investigation into where the heads were coming from, but after a lengthy inquiry an answer failed to present itself. The Colonials had their ideas certainly, citing the showers as a sure sign of the apocalypse, but in the United Kingdom, where the notion of God holds little sway, the heads were merely another in a long line of peculiar meteorological occurrences. Probably something to do with global warming. Just one of those things.

In time, reinforced parasols appeared for sale on the high street and special shelters sprung up for the benefit of those caught in a downpour. In an effort to address the inclement weather, local Councils stepped up street-sweeping initiatives to keep the highways and byways clean of rotting meat, and drains were enlarged to accommodate even the roomiest of skulls. In the event of a particularly bad spell, special ploughs were employed to bulldoze human heads to the side of the road where they'd present less of an obstruction, as had been necessary during the great head storm of 2011.

As they became more commonplace in our lives, people began to make peace with the occasional unexplained shower of human heads. Indeed, meteorological forecasts began alerting the public to any forthcoming head precipitation by introducing a new icon to their weather maps – a red emoji with a smiley face. It was a sad face at first, but people wrote in to complain. After all, nobody likes a sad face.

After a fashion

It was an unfortunate slip of the mouse that caused Dennis to accidentally purchase the model instead of the clothes she was wearing. Not that he acknowledged his error right away. In fact, he didn't realise something had gone awry until he went to collect his niece's birthday present from the post office and found a parcel waiting for him that was surely far too large to be a pink quilted sweater from River Island.

When Dennis got the package home and discovered what was inside, he was elated. An attractive young woman, a model no less, and living in his house! Surely this was every red-blooded male's dream? Yet the fantasy was to quickly turn sour.

After some painfully stilted chit-chat, Dannis fast came to understand that fashion models don't make for the most stimulating of companions. Any expectation he might have had of them being supernaturally beautiful, jet-setting glamour pusses was laid to rest the instant he saw the model slouched on his armchair champing on a stick of Wrigley's as a cow chews on cud. As for sexual desirability, climbing aboard her looked as though it would be about as much fun as straddling a bin bag full of coat hangers.

There was the issue of her age too. On the TV screen fashion models always seemed so worldly, so self-assured. Not so in the flesh.

Beneath her airbrushed tofu skin and razor-sharp cheekbones was a vacant-eyed teenage girl like any other. A grunting, brain-dead juvenile, no different to his own niece; a habitual text messager and noted mouth-breather.

It was the memory of his brother's daughter that reminded Dennis of the pink quilted sweater he'd yet to replace, so phoned River Island and explained the mix-up. Thankfully, the member of staff he spoke to was a credit to the company, offering to send him a replacement garment free of charge. He asked about returning the girl, but the lady told him the model was no longer required. Apparently they lose all value once they become domesticated.

This left Dennis with something of a predicament. The model's clacking up and down the floorboards in spike heels was driving his downstairs neighbours spare, so he'd promised to get shot of her. The trouble was, no one wanted a model; even the charity shops turned down the offer of a free mannequin. He tried adoption, but when he put an ad on Gumtree the responses he got back were far too lascivious for his liking. In a single moment of desperation he even toyed with the idea of pushing her out of his car onto the hard shoulder of the motorway, but knowing his luck she'd have found her way back using the mobile phone that was as much an accessory as the nose on her face.

Then, one day, Dennis read about a local

fashion expo and hatched a plan. Perhaps if the model was introduced to her own kind, maybe then she'd spread her wings and fly the coop. At first she took to the idea of leaving the house with the same level of eye-rolling enthusiasm she shared for a good square meal, but once she arrived at the event and saw the other models pacing up and down the catwalk, a twinkle appeared in her heavily mascara'd eye.

"Run," he said, releasing her onto native soil, "run free," and off she bounded towards the runway with the coordination of a newborn gazelle. The moment her feet took to the platform she became transformed though – her usual slovenly shuffle traded for a confident strut – her shoulders thrown back and down like a lioness prowling the veldt. Unfortunately, the wild animal analogies were to prove more apt than expected.

The catwalk models snarled and hissed at the unwelcome intrusion into their pride. Perhaps the girl had spent too long away from the wild, perhaps the catwalk models smelled human on her, but she was taken down like a buffalo at a watering hole. The spectacle was of the like rarely seen outside of a National Geographic – nimble and savage – and within minutes all that was left of the girl was a skeletonised corpse draped in scraps of bloody fabric.

Which reminded Dennis, whatever happened to that pink quilted sweater he was promised?

Show and tell

"Thank you very much for that, Malachi," said Miss Perkins, clapping and encouraging the rest of the class to do likewise.

The boy took a seat and set his banjo back in its case.

Miss Perkins checked the register. "Okay class, next up we have Katy Taylor with her favourite pet."

The kids sat up in their seats as Katy led her pet to the front of the class. Her pet Hitler.

"Oh my God," exclaimed Miss Perkins as she clapped eyes on the Austrian dictator.

"Don't worry, Miss," Katy assured her, "he doesn't bite."

Miss Perkins could hardly find the words. "Is that...?"

"Hitler is my bestest friend in the whole wide world!" said Katy, grabbing him in a bear hug.

The kids sprang from their desks, crowding around, eager to give Hitler a stroke.

"What kind of a Hitler is he, Katy?" asked Malachi, excitedly petting the dictator's moustache.

"He's a pure breed Führer," said Katy.

Miss Perkins elbowed her way through the throng of children. "Okay, I think that's enough now..."

Malachi ignored her. "Can I give Hitler a treat?" he asked Katy.

Malachi went to give Katy's pet a bite of his sandwich but Hitler caught sight of the Star of David necklace he was wearing and went berserk, straining at his leash and snapping for Hebrew flesh.

Miss Perkins rapped Hitler on the nose with a rolled up lesson plan. "That's enough! Everyone back to your seats. Katy, put your Hitler in the corner so we can continue the show and tell."

A collective groan went up from the class as they begrudgingly returned to their desks.

"Okay, time for our next show and tell," Miss Perkins went on. "Next up we have Stephen to show us his favourite toy."

Stephen wheeled a giant Jack-in-the-box to the front of the class.

"My goodness, what have you got for us there, Stephen?" asked Miss Perkins.

"This is my bestest present ever," he replied, winding the toy's crank. Moments later the lid popped open and Winston Churchill came bobbing out on a giant spring. After that it was pandemonium as Hitler snapped free from his leash and all hell broke loose.

Hardware

"Danny's mum sticks dildos up her fanny."

That's what the kids shouted at him in the playground. If only their taunts were a misrepresentation of the facts, but no. His mother stuck dildos up her fanny. Not only that, she wrote about it. For a living. She was paid to test sex toys and review them on her blog – discuss their merits, debate their value for money and grade her orgasms out of five.

Needless to say, it was an endless source of humiliation for Danny. Couldn't she write about something else? Anything else! Holiday destinations, beauty products, cruet sets, anything but inserting rubber objects into her genitalia.

Danny confronted her about it one day – explained what the kids at school were saying.

"They say you stick dildos in your fanny."

"Tell them they can say what they like," she said. "Tell them those dildos are what put food in your mouth."

Perhaps unsurprisingly, Danny did not tell them that. Instead he trotted out the time-honoured, "I wish I'd never been born," then slammed his bedroom door with a mind to give the Earth a new fault line.

Danny decided he'd had enough of the

playground taunts. If his mum wouldn't get herself a normal job he'd just have to resort to sabotage, so Danny waited until she'd gone to bed then crept into the spare room where she kept her collection. To the ottoman that had once served as his toy box but now contained her treasure trove of substitute sex organs.

Danny lifted the lid of the ottoman with a gloved hand and went to shovel its contents into a bin liner. He recoiled though as something reached back at him from within – a closed fist, black yet gleaming in the wan light. The fingers of the fist opened with a rubbery squeak and the palm set down on the edge of the box. There was a terrible groan as the arm flexed and boosted the top half of a creature from inside.

A great lolling head emerged, a sickening assemblage of dildos in every shape and size. Its tongue was a rabbit vibrator, forked and quivering with a cobra's hiss. Its barrel-like torso was a balloon animal of ribbed schlongs. Its legs a sinewy cluster of rubberised members packed tight as a tube of spaghetti. As it slithered from the ottoman and raised itself to its full height, a thick tail swished in its wake, a fused pair of double-enders.

Danny attempted to crawl away but the creature snaked out a black hand, grabbed him by the ankle and began to drag him towards the box. He clawed at the carpet but it did him no good. The creature was relentless. An unholy mélange of counterfeit phalluses that sought not to create life like their flesh counterparts, but to do the very opposite. To take life. To unmake it.

Danny used to say he wished he'd never been born. Danny was about to get the next best thing.

Destination

Bea met Greg after the War ended, at the Old
Queen's Head, back when they were young.
From across the saloon she sat and watched
him and his friends play the strangest game
of darts. Greg had folded a ten bob note three
times and pinned it to the bullseye, and the
boys were taking turns to hit it. Not just hit
it, mind you, but hit it facing the wrong
direction and firing between their legs. They'd
been going at it that way for ten minutes,
their arrows scarcely hitting the board let
alone their mark, when – spurred on by a gin
and tonic – Bea asked if she could have a go.
Greg smiled and handed her a dart. "Hit that
in one," he said, "and I'll marry you." They
were wed a month later.

Now Greg was gone and all Bea had left of
him were memories. Memories and his voice.
Greg had found work as an actor after the
War, lending his baritone to the radio shows
of the day. Over the decades his voice had
earned him lots of acting jobs –
advertisements, train platform
announcements, talking robots at faraway
theme parks – he was rarely out of work.
Right before he passed he even got to hear
his voice spoken by a brand new piece of
space-age technology, a *sat nav* they called it.

Bea stepped into the car and fastened her
belt before turning on the sat nav and
entering her destination. She listened,
smiling as Greg told her to go left, to take a

right, to travel two miles before switching to the inside lane. Eventually, after the sun had left the sky, Greg told Bea she'd arrived. She pulled over. Over to where the Old Queen's Head used to be, now long gone, now just a car park. "You have reached your destination," Greg said, and Bea felt a lump in her throat. Without turning off the engine she took a length of hose from the glove box and went to end her journey.

The Apocalypse:
a review

Plot:

Exasperated by mankind's rampant immorality, the master of disaster, God, visits destruction upon His creation.

Verdict (aka Judging Judgment Day):

And so we arrive at the deadline of human history, but to paraphrase T.S. Elliot, did it end with a whimper or a bang?

Certainly the Apocalypse comes to us with nothing less than sky high expectations. Advertised as *the* event of the season, there's simply no escaping this calamity, and a calamity it is, in every definition of the word.

Partly to blame is the cataclysm's marketing campaign, which dragged on incessantly, revealing plot details as early as the New Testament. This deluge of publicity led to a distinct sense of Apocalypse fatigue, leaving this reviewer bored to high heaven with famines, plagues and Nicolas Cage blockbusters long before the main event came to pass.

The Apocalypse's execution – both figurative and literal – is lackluster to its core. Though we were promised a chain of events that would rock our very world, the genocide of humanity proves a chore. A hodge-podge of absurdities culminating in an abrupt deus ex machina ending, it's impossible to shake the feeling that God simply phoned this one in.

Indeed, at times, one wonders if the Creator even read the source material before he agreed to stage this hopelessly dated piece. What led Him to think a 21st century audience would respond to an ancient text written by half-forgotten desert dwellers? Mel Gibson may have succeeded with *The Passion of the Christ,* but to pull that trick off twice would require nothing short of a miracle.

None of this is to say the production doesn't contain the occasional flash of brilliance. Some of the action sequences are solid for sure (the stars of Heaven falling to Earth being a definite case of Apocalypse, Wow!), but no amount of fireworks can disguise this spectacle for what it is; another cookie cutter cataclysm.

The setup, with its endless prophetic handwringing, limps through a monotonous mid-section to a third act that trots out every tiresome trope of the genre. A prime example of Revelation's unforgivable lack of, well, *revelations*, is the inclusion of not one but *four* Horsemen of the Apocalypse; a sure sign of thematic overkill. Another sin is the rote use of the walking dead, which might have seemed novel in bible times, but screams of cliché in our zombie-savvy age. The whore of Babylon puts in some credible work towards the end, but it's a case of too little too late.

179

Those who do manage to stick it out for the showstopper are in for more disappointment. When *SPOILER ALERT* Jesus makes an appearance, there's a sense that things are about to kick into another gear, but it quickly becomes apparent that what worked so well in the Gospel of Matthew is a literal tribulation the second time around. Ultimately, we learn that 'Second Coming' is just another way of saying 'Tired Sequel.'

For something that was meant to leave me in a state of rapture, it's a damning indictment that this End of Times felt as though it would never end.

Rating: *An absolute catastrophe. 1½ stars*

Bonus Material

AKA genuine lowlights from a nine-year-old file entitled 'Story_Ideas.doc' that I found on a hard drive the size of a shoe box.

- Kids literally growing up faster these days. End up older than parents.

- Bad Lieutenant. Just really incompetent at his job. Plain no good at law enforcement.

- Sexual predator exhibit at the zoo.

- A mystery disease causes people to speak medieval, mayhaps?

- Urethra Franklin.

- Detective show: Helen Keller Investigates.

- Tinky Winky keeps picking up the adult channel on his stomach.

- An illiterate child hires a hooker to read the latest Harry Potter to him.

- Victim will only speak to the press via a Christopher Walken impersonator.

- Stan Lee accidentally makes a cameo in Hotel Rwanda.

Acknowledgements

To my four horsemen, Alex Musson, Matthew Stott, David Lemon and James Rose.

To Janet Bettesworth for her words of kindness/ruthless grammatical corrections.

And to Mum and Dad, whose one and only obstacle to my childhood ambitions was to stop me digging a deathtrap dungeon in their back garden. Just so you know though, it would have been righteous.

Printed in Great Britain
by Amazon